YOUR CAIUS AQUILLA

ALSO BY JOHN ANDREW FREDRICK

the knucklehead chronicles

The King of Good Intentions

The King of Good Intentions II: The continuing & really rather quite hilarious misadventures of an indie rock band called The Weird Sisters

Fucking Innocent: The Early Films of Wes Anderson

YOUR CAIUS AQUILLA

JOHN ANDREW FREDRICK

A Rare Bird Book | Rare Bird Books
453 South Spring Street, Suite 302
Los Angeles, CA 90013
rarebirdbooks.com

Set in Centaur
Printed in the United States

10 9 8 7 6 5 4 3 2 1

Publisher's Cataloging-in-Publication data available upon request

"*Fans of Fredrick's seminal indie rock band the black watch will immediately recognize his voice: equal parts punk ethos and Wildean wit and trenchant observations on war, death, sex, and love.* Your Caius Aquilla *reads like Proust on meth by way of* A Funny Thing Happened on the Way to the Forum. *It's funny, obscene, touching, and quite unlike anything else.*"

—David Rocklin, author of *The Luminist*

"*Hystericallus majorus! A pistol of an epistolary novel. It ensnares the reader in its mordant clutches, pounding the funny bone with merciless abandon until he is spent and flummoxed as to what the hell just happened. If you read one book by an author with three names, make sure it's this one.*"

—Bruce Ferber, author of *Cascade Falls*

"*The hilarious and seamless mix of conversational affectations from ancient Rome, modern America, and any place in-between makes the characters feel timeless. You'll laugh, you'll cry—well, you might not cry; you'll likely just laugh some more. This novel's simply stunningly imagined.*"

—Dave Coverly, *Speed Bump* cartoonist

"Unprovided with original learning, unformed in the habits of thinking, unskilled in the arts of composition, I resolved to write a book."

—Edward Gibbon

For Nora

In our relentlessly Romance-obsessed era it's rather hard for many of us to fathom how other epochs could and did prize friendship over love. A Roman legionnaire, for instance, in writing home to his beloved wife would invariably address her as "Dear Friend" rather than Wife or Her Name. Here's a sample letter home—from the Sixteenth Punic War or something. Translated from the Latin.

XII FEBRUARIUS

Dear Friend:

Hail! I hope this missive finds you healthy and well. We sure have slain no small amount of Germans, Spaniards, Saxons, or Goths this week! *Whew!* I'm *so* tired. I can barely lift my sword arm over my effin' head—pardon my Gallic. It's been nothing but march, march, march, kill, kill, kill this entire campaign: none of your "hearts and minds" palaver and nonsense at all this time for sure. I don't know what the higher higher-ups are thinking but the venerable generals are *not* in the least effing around here. Around they are decidedly not effing. Not this particular show, that's certain. Thank Mars and Jove it's almost over. Got any idea how hard it is to cut off a guy's head when your weapon's smeared with blood from a Franctk's (spelling?) jugular or the neck of a Pict and it's your third or fourth head that day that's had to be cut off? And—thusly cutting and thrusting and beheading—you haven't had an iota of time to fetch a nice new blade or have one of the smiths at the smithy sharpen your old one for you while you hurriedly refresh yourself with muddy or bloody river water or a squirt of watered wine? Forgive me, dear friend, for nattering on and on about work. How are you, anyway? And the kids? How I long for the warmth of Rome and your arms. How I dream of you—and of you taking me into your mouth, dearest friend. Good gods I'm almost ready to go Greek as it were and have one of the slave camp boys suckle my aching julius! But no. I don't really mean that. Only joking. That only happened that one time, I swear by all the gods and lesser goddesses; and as you know I sacrificed two goats and a chicken in penance to Diana and a calf to Venus so... Well, anyway. I hardly know what I am scribbling here, I'm so worn out from today's fray. You must indulge me, forgive me. Only too well do I know, Lora, that you wouldn't like that if I did that, I'm sure. I mean, *I* would like it—don't get me wrong. But you, you wouldn't. So I'm not going to—rest assured. I swear by Janus's faces I won't and may I roam in the darkest depths of lowest Hades always if ever again am I even tempted to do such a sordid, sorrow-making thing. Instead, ergo, every night I as I take my desperate scepter in hand and pull myself off I envision coming home and luxuriating in a good hot Roman bath, then snacking on barbecued larks' wings, your most excellent and still mighty perky breasts, and the greatest pizza known to man. I say! I'll try to port you home some different spoils this time, my love. How's that?! I'll bet you anything you're tired as Hades of feigning delight when I bring back a baby monkey or a necklace made of jade, lapis lazuli, and the teeth of a Celtic child. And the kids are totally all, like, "*Another* primate, Daddy? What are you/can you be *think*ing? If thinking at all. The stupid compound courtyard's starting not only to look but to *sound* like a zoo!..." By the by, in case you're wondering, I'm still sharing a blasted tent with Beeflicus. You can imagine how much fun *that* is after we've dined, say, on heaps of fresh cow and he's had a goblet or two (or four). Picture this, if you would be so kind: there I am the other night, on my cot reclining, taking my ease after a long day, tacitly practicing my lute, and Beefy up and smiles his wily smile and smirks right at me and just rips one—a good, long, jarringly jabbering blast from his fat arse—and I says to him I says, "Godsdammit, Beefy old man, you're a deuced, impudent blackguard, and if you don't stop making this tent bellow like the sails of a swift Sicilian ship, and smelling like an Abyssinian bog, I am going to cut your sorry throat in the dead of night!" Some of the other lads have noticed (and how could they not?) his bloody proclivity for stupendous and dramatically sustained flatulence and have dubbed him "Lower Aeolus" and/or "Aeolus from Below." They call that clever. They call that hilarious. I call it appalling. Utterly unacceptable. Mark this, love, no lie, I have to sleep with a wet rag over my nose. The other day Joculator asked Lieutenant Optio if, next attack, we couldn't have young Beefs *march backward* so as to "beef out" the enemy, so to speak, like a phalanx of rank skunks, before we get to them. Everyone busted up like you wouldn't believe. Everyone but me, that is. Waggish Joc tried to get him (i.e. Beefy) to rip one right then to show the clearly bemused officer what he (Joc) meant, but Beef couldn't manage it. He wasn't in the mood, I guess. "Come on, Beefy," Joc cajoled, "be a good boy and show the lieutenant what you can do!" "I've been straight plumb downwind of him, sir," someone whose voice I didn't recognize shouted from way far behind me in the ranks, "and I should wager two campaign's worth of salary that he could take out an entire first wave with just one blast! Just one, I'm telling you, and he could open a hole in their ranks wide as the Appian Way!" "Just give him a plate of Gauls' mess and he's good to go!" Marcellus chimed in. "Not funny," yelped I. "*You* chaps try being his tent mate for just one night!" I got a few chuckles and maybe five titters before Joc trumped me and got off a really good one: "I'd sooner face a thousand breakfastless Etruscans—and me unshielded!" Everyone roared, nothing but complete cachinnation and fond, broad grins for the royal wit Joculator. Beefy smiling smirkily. Me sort of scowling but trying not to. All this, and you *know* how I abominate *any* sort of scatological humor and think it's positively revolting! Oh, well. Look after yourself. Be well. Eat well. As in please don't get fat. Last time I campaigned... Well, you know. Let's not have to go through that again. Hit the gymnasium *now*, please, darling. Don't wait. I know how you are. Minute I'm out the door you've three thick stalks of sugar cane in your gob; then you start in on the candied almonds, and wash it all down with wine after wine after wine. Gods know *I'm* keeping fit, in shape. Do your part, as well. Try to be of good cheer during my absence. I think you sport eat because you miss me so much. Bananas, it was, last time—remember? Fruit really packs on the poundage. Try and have some self-control. Eat pig and cow—those are far and away the best substitutes for all those sweetmeats and puddings, cookies, and cakes. Jellied eel: there's another, better snack for you, Lora. How we Romans love the flesh of that delicious delicacy! Ye gods what I wouldn't give right now for a platter of the stuff. How yum would *that* be! Best not to think on't. Yet trying not to think about it, and all the other foodstuffs you can't get on campaign, only makes one crave them more and more and more, sooth to say. Ah, irony. Goodbye for now, dear friend. Take care. I miss you, you know, very much. I can't wait to see you (if you've not ballooned, that is). Kidding! You know I have a wicked wicky-wacky sense of humor. If I survive long enough to retire from the Legion I may even try doing a bit of stand-up. Hie me down to the Forum and give it a go. Maybe. I don't know. Probably not. I'm inclined to think it's only one of my little velleities, little vanities. I'm sure I'd chicken out, back out, suffer terrible, dreadful, horrible stage fright. Imagine that! Me having stage fright. Isn't that funny? No qualms meeting an hoard of half-naked, ululating, armed-to-the-teeth Persians but frightened as a rabbit at the prospect of getting up in front of an audience. Quaking in my battle sandals. That's me all over, though. Quite keen in theory, vacillating at the actual prospect. We all have dreams, I imagine. And whether or not they turn to account, turn into realities, is anybody's or the gods's guess, don't you know. *Sigh.* Nevertheless, before you know it we'll be together again, wife. I do so very look forward to that. You can advise me, Lora. I can try out my routine—if I ever get one together—on you and the children. Er, or maybe just you, seeing as some of the material I'm thinking of working up isn't exactly appropriate for Under-XVIII's. Tell you what: when I get home, I'm going to "perform" (if you know what I'm saying) for you like you've never seen! Until we meet (how sweet!) again, I am

Your Caius Aquilla

P.S. Try to get tickets for the Coliseum a couple of months from now for when (if?) I come back. Strangely, having seen so much otiose bloodshed and mayhem, I jones for it whenever I come back. Rotating back to the world (i.e. Rome; an "Army expression" if there ever was one), I'll miss it, surely—that adrenalin rush, that thrill of swift and sudden violence and slaughter and all of that. It's like a high that's hard to come down from, killing and warring. You'd think it'd be quite the opposite—that I would be sick to death, sick at heart, of gore and GBH and stuff—but weirdly enough that's not the case at all. It's doubtless a sort of an addiction.

P.P.S. If the Legion doesn't make it back in time you can always have one of the servants scalp them, the tickets, that is—not the servants. Ba-da-bing, ba-da-boom! Rim shot, rim shot, rim shot.

P.P.P.S. Guess what? Beeflicus just beefed a*gain*, lifting brazenly his left leg straight *at me* like a German salute. A long, staccato then legato blast in E flat, if I'm not mistaken. Tell a lie: F major 7. Now I'm going to scalp *him*, for the gods' sake! I can't take this anymore! He's *laughing*. He won't for long, though. Pah! Stinks to the highest skies in here now. Thanks, Beef! Real sweet. Some chum you are.

P.P.P.P.S. Oh! The E flat or rather F major 7 comment reminded me: how are your harp lessons going?!

Editor's note: Well, guess what? We've unearthed the entire correspondence. Tell a lie: we can't say the entire in case some of the letters have gone missing or were burned or lost in the post or got singed by an angry volcano or eaten by an idiotic yard dog. Nevertheless, if you've enjoyed Caius Aquilla's style and content (as we certainly have; gotta hand it to him—he is pretty funny, witty, charming, etc.), here are quite a few more epistles for your enjoyment, delectation, or amusement, not forgetting wife Lora Caecilia's return missives:

XIII FEBRUARIUS (or sometime thereabouts)

Drear Freind:

Beefy's dead. Poor fool. Poor bastard. I'm drunk. Positativily legless. (Sorry, spelling's gone out straight the window, even though no widow do we have here but tent flap opening which isn't.) I'll try to and sober up a bit. Not easy. So wasted. Plus it's loud out. Kinda deafning, in fact. Almost the entire regiment's reeling round the shambled encampments, arm in arm and singing or waving crazy faces in each other's torches and behaving like slaves on holiday or barbarians any day. *Victory is ours! Hail Caesar! Romulus, Rebus, rah, rah, rah! The Seventh till the dreaming Fields of Elysium* and all of that rubbish. Well, they can't be faulted, I reckon, can't be blamesed for suchlike carry-on: we won a big one today. Six thousand or so of us against maybe seven or eight at the hundred most of raggle-taggle, scattershot them. Just a wipe-out. A pitiful show. Totally one-sided. Over in a flash—they never hit what knew them. Some of these clashes just seem so bloody unfair: what should just be a minor skirmish turns into a major rout. But I reckon Jove's sent them us (these breezes, these occasional cinchy mop-ups) to make up for all the Pyrrhic ones we had in inexpressibly execrable Africa. Those were no joke. Losses galore. Very heavy. Maybe it's Mars's doing, I don't know. I'm sick of those Pyrrhic ones, nevertheless. At one point today, looking across the glorious red and marigold field of dubious battle, I thought: "I bet you I could actually *count* the enemy over there." Their side looked so scrappy, so scrawny, and us of course as per usual cutting a dash like mad in full beautiful scarlet and gold Imperial regalia. And them resembling a bunch of wooly hairy dirty barbarian gibberish-hollering guys out hunting who just happened upon (into?) the teeth of the mighty Seventh Roman Legion! Not the teeth literally. But in the sense of...oh, you know what I mean. So drunk here. Don't think I've have ever been so! Steady, steady. OK. So there we spot them, this morning sometime, I think it was, our newly-polished silver armor clanking fierce and percussive in the morning sun as the mists lifted, the crunch contrasting very with the soft whoosh of our swift sandals going over the wet heather, the threshing of our marching calves brushing scratchy purple thistles. "Oh, *shit*, oh *fuck!*" I thought I heard one of them, the enemy, say—an eerie echo echoing over the echoing field—as we flanked them, then wedged up into regulation square formation, then smashed through them in the flash of a knife, don't you know, like a warm spoon going into a bowl of cooled, quivering golden egg custard. Oh it was smooth, went as smooth, as one's palm waving like the very air over leafs, or sheaves of bowing wheat as one wends one's way through a dewy field of it at evening in mellowest amber springtime, under canopies of colored cloud; smooth as one sliding on one's trusty round *arma* down a happy grassy knoll or dell or dingle, zipping round like so many orange and purple butterflies in ripefullest spring. The trumpets trumpeted triumphantly, the venerable generals bravely waved and nodded to the proud officers and narrowed in glorious knowingness and acknowledgement their watchful eyes, the officers proudly shouted grimly-smiling/teeth-gritting orders to advance and, in sum, victory was ours, was everyone's! Yes, yes, yes, yes! Hurrah, hooray, hurrah! Hooray, hey up, hurrah! Huzzah! Everyone's, victory was! Well, everyone's but Beefy's. Poor fellow. Poor guy. His was a sad defeat, a bad end. You know how yesterday I wrote to tell you I was contemplating slitting his throat and everything? For all his brazen you-know-what? Well, now I don't *have* to, Pluto be praised. A massive patch of horrid vomit-colored quicksand saved me the trouble. Not that I was going to take it, the trouble, that is. You do know that, right, my love? You know I wasn't being serious? Wouldn't hurt him if he asked me to, begged me to. Poor Beefy. Poor beggar. Here's what happened: Oh, Hail, by the way. Did I say that yet? Hope you're doing well. And, yes, I miss you still— even more than I did in yesteradays's posting. OK, though, lisssen up, lisssten here, my darling dear. I really should probably have a wee lie-down before I continue to writing this, really. Now me head's going off like fireworks on a merry-go-round. Have you ever had a sore head—also known as "a hangover" or as a "katzenjammer" (a Saxon word I learned the other day)—*while you were drinking?* I have. I have that right now, in fact. It's no fun at all. Funny thing, though: all these years we've been together and I've never asked you that. And do I ever know how you like to knock back a drink or two! Gods know I do, too. One of the many reasons I married you: 'cause you're great to drunk with. Get drink with, I mean. Drunk. Oh my propitious constellations, I'm personally haven't been this plowed since I honestly don't know when. Day before yesterday, maybe. Kidding. Kind of. I'm toasted. Com*pletely* pissed. We've been drinking and carousing all afternoon. All us have, even the grumpy generals in all their pomp and garish-beautiful royal imperial purple cloaks and their splendiferous, beautiful-fitting, minimal armor; even the irascible, overly serious captains and the lieutenants of course and many of the aide or aides de camp or camps, if you can believe that. All drunk as skunks. Wasto. Sauced as all get-out. Discipline's gone completely the way of Atalantis (sp?). Ever seen a drunken ten-year-old? A post-toddler tippling tipsily? I should hope not. Gone completely wild, a veritable Riot Club, some of these camp boys and young lads. Unreal, rather. Absolutely appalling. I call that not funny. Lots of chaps, however, laugh like mad when a too-tipsy tyke of a camp boy goes running, making a beeline for the tree line, hugging his tummy with one hand, covering his gob with the other, rushing bushward to horf his paltry little guts out. Me, I don't at all find that funny. I say! People do have different ideas. Imagine our dear little Aurelian pickled on rank plonk and heaving a pony-sized cutlass around irresponsibly, like it was nothing, like he'd never received an ounce of training?! The thought of the very of it. Shameful. Imagine how all the whoops and assorted sounds of wassailing and victorious merrymaking sounded to the poor unfortunates in the surgeons' tents (the wounded, in other words)! Guy's had his ear pierced and scorched to absolute bits by an errant flaming arrow or his godsdamned sword hand lopped off in the heat of it, the thick of it; he's sitting there agog and incredulous, looking with absolute horror and dismay at an awful hole in his horrid red and oozy thigh the size of plump-ripe plum or tree-sweet apricot or young-green coconut; or the surgeon's just told him he's sorry to say but there's just no other way, he'll have to lose the leg, hacking it off's the only option—and said poor fellow has to hear the jubilant strains of the other lads gleefully gargling Chablis, rose, or a nice table wine and clapping one another on the hearty, good-show-old-chap back and all that rot? Jumping up and down and pounding their perfectly chiseled chests like apes or drunken Visigoths, Ostrogoths, or Lithuanians? I can't believe the callous attitudes that swirl round here, don't you know. Bloody tragic, truly. Walking back toward the mess wagons in search of a snack to settle my stomach *I came across two guys effing flogging, if you can believe that.* They were just standing there with their willies out, waving them round in the breeze, going at it—*flog, flog, flog, fap, fap, fap*—right by where the horses are tied up. Isn't that incredible? Isn't that unconscionable? How slack. How very. Full on decline of the Roman Empire or what? "Oi!" I says. "You lot! What in the name of Venus do you think you're doing?" They just laughed at kept at it. "Ah, gods, you guys—are you kidding me? Well done! Well *done!* Nice one!" I says as I trot by, averting my eyes, or trying to, at least. "NO FAT CHICKS!" one of them yelped, cracked, right at me. What the Hades was that supposed to mean, I wondered? "What the Hades does *that* mean?" I said. But they just kept on laughing, threw their silly heads back, and carried on wanking as a murder of crows cackled in the trees like some sort of musical accompaniment to their onanistic shenanigans ("shenanigans": Celtic word I heard someone who'd been to Londinium on campaign use, meaning "no-goodness or something like that; trickery; tomfoolhardiness and such"). I reckon campaigning's all just one big plethoric joke to some of these fellows. A circle jerk of *two*? Seriously, lads? Disgusting. I mean, two's not even a circle. It's, like, a dialectic or a polar opposite or a see-saw or something. It was all I could do to stagger past this grotesque burlesque. Unbelievable. Sad. Hardly befitting our ethics, the complete Roman motif. Though I suppose one might let them (i.e. the in-tandem masturbators) off the hook a wee little bit, what with all the unalloyed inebriation going round, withal: I mean, every time one's tankard got to even near the halfway mark some blasted peg-or-barrel-carrying roisterer with a makeshift laurel on his head (made of a cropped robin's or bluebird's nest or something) came crazy-legging by and splashed more and more into it and ran off guffawing. If you put your hand over the dancing mouth of it, the brim, as if to say "Cease, roisterer! No more! Away, I say!" the wine stewards and random gregarious fellows just went ahead and flung it in anyway, promiscuously, liberally, right over one of your mitts, slopping the old grape about like so many ancient charwomen tossing pots of bilge water on grimy, unscrubbed flagstones. Never once, never once in my puff have I born witness to such Bacchus-like revelry and whatnot. There was no escape from it, really. Join in or risk ostracism, 'twas. So by the end of the day, I was sticky as fresh tree gum, vine-varnished all over. You could lick just half of me and probably get drunk or at least quasi tipsy. Absurd. I don't know what gets into them sometimes, the fellows. Sometimes, truly I wonder if we're not just a gang of, a myriad of, hooligans, n'er-do-wells, and bloody common thieving rowdies ruled by pompous potentates (the generals, that is; humorless as Jews or scowling Phonecians). To which you may now add (us, i.e.) drunkards, wastrels, philistines, and well-dressed/in-shape vagabonds. How nice, eh? How very very nice. To crown all, you wouldn't hardly recognize me right now, I don't think, dear dear friend, if you saw me, which you won't, on account of I am miles and miles from Rome and home. I mean, *I* didn't recognize me at all just now. After I nibbled on a wee bit of a crust of bread and a fruit or two I went to throw a splash of water on me face to try and sober up a bit so I could write to you. As I'm looking into the basin or whatd'yecallit trough or standing bath I'm sort of screwing up my eyes (they must be red by now as a smith's face or as Rhenish wine and sore as vinegar), I go "Who *is* that chap? I know that bastard. I've seen his fat face somewhere before; I know I have." And turns out it was *me*... Me, me, me. Quite the shock. More later.... Must sleep... All right. Hey. Hail again. Hello, there. Took break. Back now. Hail/hello. Slept it off. Woke up a tad refreshed and it's only six of the clock, six thirty. Egads! Been quite dark since four, maybe four thirty. Oh, the banality. Of war, of everything. The boring boredom. Dreadful place, wherever on earth we are. *Brittany*, someone said it's called. What a strange name. Have the kids show you it on a map. If it's even there. I've never heard of it. Never know where I am, hardly. Someone said Champaign-sur-le-Lac-sur-le-Foret-d'Odette-du-Plessey or summat like that and I just thought the bloke'd sneezed a prodigious sneeze of some sort, like a stage sneeze or sumfink, like he was choking on some soup. The sounds you hear, so odd, so catch-as-catch-can, from these various alien peoples! So many of them, their vile languages, recall someone yakking profusely into a reverberant vomitorium, or a deaf mute being strangled with a belt, rope, or precious necklace. And what is *up* with these silly effing foreign names? I never bother. Paying attention, that is. Trying them out in your mouth, they only end up hurting your tongue somehow. Learning them— please! Give me a break! And what's the difference, anyway? There's never any time for language-learning on campaign as we incontrovertibly are hump-hump-humping away on a daily basis. March here, camp there, break your fast in the morning, fall in formation, pass muster, fight-fight-fight, lunch break, skirmish (maybe), play a bit of Smear the Queer or a little football (*yuck!*), take tiffin (salt and bread, plonk, and an apple that looks like your great aunt after she's fallen asleep in the bath), go on plunder detail, sort through the pillage detail, collect the wounded detail, do a bit of lightsome torturing of any captured enemy, sponge bathe, clean up, tea time, meetings-meetings-meetings, light drills and inspection, second wash off, dinner time/mess hall in an open field, wash-up, campfire or do what some like I do: practice music and write these little merry-melancholy letters home to the loved ones. Oh! Speaking of music... Well, a kind of music... The lads—in jest—made up a song about me. Let me see if I can remember how it goes. It was very sing-songy, and you can just picture them roaring over it, thinking it such a larf. They sang it, nay, *roared* it, in galloping III/IV time, mind, as I loped by just a little while ago, hurriedly, toward the steaming latrines: *Caius Aquilla—looks like a gorilla/ye gads don't he smell like one, too/Let's put him in a cage/ although he will rage/until we can get him to the zoo!* The rest of it went something like "Caius Aquilla, a something something killa, he slays them by the dozen or two, he dit dit doot do, and doo doo doo doo *doo*, still smells like a primate, too." Or something like that. It's a pretty catchy little ditty—I'll give it that. I found myself humming it all afternoon and smilingly. Ah, music, sweet music! How it transports one/me. Music of any sort does—even a vulgar camp song, and one that makes fun of one. Quite curious, that. How I miss making music with you, Lora. Speaking of places, landmarks and vistas, runes and stuff—there's never time for any sightseeing/seeing the sights. Never. None at all. As we're the elite we go in last, you know—so on the road in to base camp there's invariably been an advance force there burning and pillaging, pillaging and burning, living it up, with occasional obligatory crucifixions and rapes, authorized or unauthorized as the case may be. Some sights, those; real sweet. "Join the Army of Imperial Rome and See the World," the new recruitment motto goes. You've no doubt noted the mosaic posters round town of a centurion pointing straight at you with his sword, holding up the dripping, severed bearded head of a ghastly, crazy-looking "barbar" in his other hand. The join part is spot on, but the see the world? Yeah, sure; yeah, right. The only sights *I* ever see, it seems, are of the fat or not-fat butt of the chump humping in front of me in an insanity of sun on one of our interminable marches or in an attack-square; and the aftermath of blurry and blood-spattered battlefields, through visored metal and stinging sweat, in as I said sick-making, dizzying heat after hours upon hours of torturing boredom. Some sights! Some world! Our sailors, the navy, they tell tall tales of sirens and gorgons and Medusas and furious giants lobbing rocks from lofty and mythopoeic precipices, gargantuan insatiate sea monsters and armies of almond-eyed, smoky-eyed island girls of lissome dark beauty bearing frankincense and myrrh and steaming plates of smoked oysters and mussels and crab and lobster and scallops, plus flagons of winking-cool wine and sweet lime and lemon barley water. But we landlubber legionaries never see such dishes, have such quintessences of things to drink, nor get to gaze on such strange and/or wondrous sights. Galling, is what it is. That and no more. It's the same old same old for us grunting ones on the ground—"ground troops," I reckon you could call us. Curious phrase, that. And indeed some of us do end up on the ground, literally (dead, I mean, perish the thought and touch wood and all of that.) And ground up, as in shredded wounded. Aye, that happens, you can't deny it. And speaking *again* of sights, I meself must be such an one, a right spectacle: for my helmet keeps slipping down on account of all the sweat I sweat in the ferocious frays. See what you make of this, in fact: I keep asking the bloody fussy effing silly tight-assed and pilular quartermaster—begging him, actually, almost every day I do—to have a heart and stuff and "req" me a newer tighter spiffier helmet but they only send me over to the undersmiths, who point me back to the poxy Q'master, who gives me a chit for the smiths, who expostulate with me and fake like they're about to brand me with their red-hot tongs and irons, then shoo me straight back to you-know-who... I call that a real runaround. "Oi, Caius—ever tried wearing a cloth of some sort over your head to likesay steady your cover, make it fit good and tight and proper? Like that rag you said you put over your hooter at night?" one of the callous blacksmiths, taking the major piss, razzed the other day. How'd he know I do/did that? I wonder. The quartermaster just laughed and laughed when he heard that one. He's this very tall, very not dark, and quite desperately handsome guy Brutus—guy who I *thought* was my friend and ally and buddy. Some chum, him. Some pal. He's a ginger, so I reckon he gets made fun of quite a lot himself. Ragged on royally. Ginger's not quite the word for it, though—actually, he's *orange*. You've never seen anyone more orange. His hair's orange, his skin, even his freckles have an orange-ish hue. I'm tempted to say his eyes are even so but I wouldn't swear it. At six foot four or five he's kind of a gentle giant, and so good at quartermastering, so good with his hands—they're appropriately large and remarkably exquisite—that he's never seen combat, ever ever. They don't want to risk him getting hurt or killed or maimed on account of maintaining the armory is so important and they (whoever "they" are) are convinced he's the best that's ever lived at making and keeping sharp our swords and spears and battle axes and all that muck. That popular opinion and consensus has given him a bit of a chip on his orange shoulder, I daresay. Still, the crack about the rag, and Beefy and stuff—well, he couldn't have expected me to brook that without a retort or riposte, a way of getting back at him for laughing and keenly at my being made fun of by one of his understaff. 'Twas one of my better zingers, actually. I says to him I says: "Should you ever find yourself *by mistake* and after all this time in *one* of the frays [note my irony here], Brutus m'boy, I reckon the barbarians you'd be having a go at would freak out and run away before you even got to them on account of, *looking at you, they'd think they were being attacked by a tangerine!* Ha!" I really cracked me up on that one, dear. "Very funny," Brutus said. "Ho, ho, ho." Some people—they just can't take a joke. Not if you hand it to them on a platter, on a silver salver. Boom-chicka-bam-bam. Rim shot! Rim shot! Flatulent sound. *I* can take a joke, all right. *I* can. I've had to. Boy, have I ever. I've even been *considered* one on more than one unmerry occasion. Can you credit it? Me, one of the I daresay bravest of the brave. In a fray, you know. Oh well, nevertheless, my poor helmet. Poor old thing. Rather emblematic of the man who wears it, innit. Sports it. You couldn't brush a senator's pate with what's left of the sorry, tatty, catawampus plume. Get it? Most senators being *baldies* and all! Ha! It's seen so much combat, my jolly old lid, that the darn plume's about the width of a small boy's toothbrush. Helmet makes the man, the old saw goes. Mine's a sorry wreck and no joke. Of course, the "plume" I make reference to here is purely imaginary, totally fictitious, all just part of my comedy stich: us or we grunts's helmets aren't in the slightest adorned with those dandy red or brown brushes, more's the pity; those are for officers only, damn them for a bunch of attractive dandies, what with their insignias and broaches and fine capes of robust purple and gold clasps and many silver rings a-finger, plus all the superb eagle motifs they bedeck and bedizen themselves with. You'd think, being around them, you were in a metal aviary! Their better-made sandals, their meticulous/better haircuts and clean shirtsleeves! Oh, darling. Oh, loved one. Oh my precious wondrous lovely plump but not quite zaftig beloved. I miss you so. I love you so. So very so. I am so woe…begone right now! My dulled red heart yearns with all its blood for your presence in my absence; my strained loins cry out for the light touch of your fine, soft, fat hands. My meagre and poor prose stretches itself thin in quest of a new metaphor or simile for my yen for you. My soul—if such there be— screams "Lora, Lora, Lora, etc." Nearly my every thought is of you. You, you, you. When I'm not thinking about lunch or my helmet. Where was I? Oh, yeah—Beefy. Oh, would you mind, if you wouldn't mind, highlighting with a lick or tick of cadmium yellow or at least underscoring some of the quippier stuff and the one-liners in my letters? And checking for anachronisms? Not sure, but I wonder if I mightn't cull some material from some of these epistles for use in my…what I was telling you about in terms of my ambitions—my *perhaps* ambitions, wink, wink, nudge, nudge, poke, poke, Bronx cheer, raspberry—when I come home. Thanks in advance. Here's one, in fact, that I thought up the other day—see if you think this one's up there with some of my better jibes, jests, and all- round jokes: "An actress walks up to the director of the play she's in and says: 'Well, as an *artist* I…'" What do you think?! That one just came to me today as we were double-timing it toward the battlefield. Isn't it odd how the creative process works? You can just be trotting off to slay some infies, or standing in the queue for mess, or innocently farming your nose in your tent when no one's looking, and suddenly—*boom!*—a great joke or idea descends on you like the sword of Damocles! I hope you like it. I do. I keep trying out new ways of saying it, the delivery and that. I love it. Cracks me up to no end. Have told it to a few of the guys but—I dunno—they're not exactly the most sophisticated crowd. Not surprised such a zinger came to me whilst ambulating. Nothing like a good hike for inspiration and all of that rubbish. It's said that good old hoary Socrates thunk up a lot of the profound stuff he thunk up whilst on his walks (i.e. constitutionals) around the Parthinaan (sp?), which indubitably eventuated in his entelechy. Remind me, do, to take a few good, swift Socratic strolls when I come home, won't you? Some bracing jaunts on shank's pony, take a few turns around the streets of our superbly walled and not exactly neighborly neighborhood. I don't need much reminding here on campaign on account of we do so much hiking, marching, running, trekking, what-have-you while we're working, you see. But at home I know I am wont to neglect to exercise and just lounge around all day reading such trash as crosses my writing desk and as tickles my fancy and sucking down stalk upon stalk of sugar cane, glugging fine wine with you, and playing with the kids and feasting like a starveling, plus of course (as is only meet and right to do) waiting for you to be in the right mood to let me have you, fairly ravish you. Ravishing you—oh is that not just a nice and torturing thought, Lora, Lora, Lora. Having just the one portrait of you (I keep it with me always, dear; right inside my breastplate), I have to strain hard sometimes to picture your gorgeous Loraface. Catullus the artist's drawing isn't a great likeness, I don't think. I don't think it does your considerable beauty justice. I flicked it out a few weeks ago as the lads were passing round pics of their sweethearts and, handling yours, garrulous Joculator goes "Oi, who's *this* cove, mate? He looks like a chimp or—whatyoucallit—orangutan!" Thanks a lot, Joc. Nice one. Real nice. He got (again!) just a load of laughs outta that one. See what I mean about them (the lads, that is) not exactly appreciating the finer points of subtle humor? Last time I ever show anybody your portrait, Lor. 'Twill be a secret, between my breast and me (it's in a locket, you know). Oh! If only I could see you right now, hold you, kiss you, touch you, palpate your fine skin, your bum and haunches, tummy, thighs, etc. But just to look at you, dear friend: content I'd be. The sight of you (who decidedly do not look like a chimp or orangutan, okay?) would be the most welcome thing in all gods's creation. Just spectacular. Come to think of it, speaking of seeing things and stuff, we do sometimes see something worth seeing out here amidst all the phantasmagoria of war and all. About a mile out, e.g., from base camp just t'other day there was this vast, nice field of beautiful bluebells—just miles and miles or at least a hundred yards of them— nodding next to acres of canting reeds amidst plosive heather and a smattering of cornflowers glittering in the sun. Absolutely utterly simply breathtaking, it was—and then even more so as, all of a sudden, hundreds of lovely butterflies emerged from nowhere, then married in the pollen- filled air. A bit farther (further?) on we come upon great patches of celandine and eglantine and cyclamen, daisies and chrysanthemums, then thistles galore, exploding with tart, splendiferous, purplish, splashy color near some soughing wheat fields, that sighed surreally, like they were some strange, living thing, eerie and queer with quiet and ominous portentousness—yet absolutely rivetingly pretty, arresting somehow, like something you see and just wonder at the world, its wonderfulness and majestic charm. A bit on from there, there were low snowy mountains in the blue-blue distance, and tall, incredible curds-and-whey clouds in a painted sky unlike I've ever seen. A congeries of chestnut trees, cherry trees, almond trees near green streams. Marching as the crow flies we made for some gently rolling meadows crisscrossed with more brilliant- tiered rivulets of diaphanous green, hyacinths abounding, water lilies, orchids, sunflowers, bluebells, yellow/red/white roses, lilac, sweet William, Johnny-jump-ups, birds-of-paradise, nasturtiums, and lilies of the valley. Then onto dirt-pink silt-soft parallel thoroughfares, dotted with innumerable buttercups, daisies, and peonies on either side. Astonishing. Ah. Wondrous. Nature. Stupendously splendiferous. Quiet shadows with splashes of splotchy sunshine. Marvelous sights. Calming, beatific. The very thing. Lovely. Okay, so: the Beefy thing. Here's the deal. Okay. Might as well come right out with it—tell it to you straight, my dear. What happened was… Oh, this is hard, so hard. I'm a bit choked up here; hard indeed it is to keep a stiff upper lip and all of that. I can hardly believe he's gone. Can't believe he's dead, godsdammit. I'll try and buck up, I'll do my level best; I'm all but gutted here and no mistake. All told, he was my mate and tent mate, and we saw a goodly amount of action together, gods rest his gaseous soul. Okay. So we go patrolling after today's big show—strictly routine, utterly quotidian, nothing to get your knickers in a twist about, nothing we haven't done an hundred and seven times before, even though it's what we call being "in the shit." On account of anything can happen, retaliation-wise. It's a mop-up sort of sortie down these long lush green glens beside a marsh behind some woods near a town on a lake abutting a rivulet past some waterfalls next to a mountainside. I say a lake but it's a big pond, really. A lakelet at *best*. A g.d. *swamp* if you were in no mood to be generous or conciliatory, geographically speaking. After the massacre (when the archers are "on," boy is our job a lot easier; the hardest thing we have to do is keep from being singed by one of the cloaks of a still-burning enemy, or mowed down by one of our own cavalry, the huzzah-crying horsemen) I say, we split up into patrols and went through the strangely quiet villes and silly little hamlets to check and see if there were any cowering cowards hanging about, hiding down wells or in hovels or in hutches or in attics or atop some of the larger oaks and pine trees and that, under patchy hatches covered by crude rugs and stuff in stinky old huts; trying to disguise themselves as ugly old beldams in tatty cloaks or whatnot. There you are, moving out along, say, a trail where there's a sharp shelf of pale brown or pink rock, and out pops two or three of them, just like—*snap!*—that, flinging great rocks at you or a chucking a spear that wobbles right toward then past (or maybe not past) your godsforsaken breastplate. They can be so sly, sometimes, these people. So devious and resilient. You really gotta watch it. Keep an eye out always. They're animals, basically. That's really all they are: not-human creatures. Very crafty, and quite often replete with malice aforethought and ruthlessness. You've got to watch out for them as you would a nasty snake or rabid-mad child or infuriated drunken woman who's just found out that you've been untrue to her with multiple partners, some of whom she's acquainted with or related to. The enemy! You don't know what they're going to do, what to expect. Beneath their sometimes smiling eyes—such malicious intent. And these overt aggressions—it goes without saying—will not stand. We're fighting for *freedom* here. And glory, of course. That's what we're told, anyway. The freedom and the glory of the peoples we are quote-unquote teaching to love Rome, adapt or adopt Roman ways, Roman values, Roman…other stuff we stand for. So that they can be free to be our servants, to bow down to us, their ineluctable masters, and to Rome itself. Which only makes sense. Do you see the logic? I must admit it's hard for me to work it out; it's a paradox. Yes, that's it. A paradox. We enslave the ones we don't kill so that they can have the privilege of living/loving Rome. It's wonderful. And rather self-explanatory, in a paradoxical way, I suppose. Interesting, though. Very. Looked at like that, as a statement of our "mission" in going on these "missions," you really see the beauty and selflessness of the conquering "enterprise," the manner in which it reveals our benevolent intentions toward these valueless pagans and barbarians. They'll have the chance—well, they'll be forced, actually—to worship our gods (the right gods, naturally) and adopt or adapt to our customs and mores. That's pretty righteous, *I* think. What do I know, though? What I know. That's all. I'm just doing my duty, serving my city-state, keeping the faith, fighting the good fight, keeping my pecker up, making sure morale doesn't flag, that my brothers-in-arms are making sure the body count's on the upswing so that the stats look good, work out, keep us out of the brig or the clink or what-have-you. *Semper fi.* One for all and all for Rome. So anyway, came we upon a long house sort of job/thing, plain and made of twigs and branches and thatched with straw. Cut grass in bunches, clusters—tussocks is what you call them, methinks—outside it, and piles of stacked pink rocks and slats of schist and yellowish brown bricks, and scaffolds of hewed logs braced against the blackened building, a little citadel or rather an abode. An abode I shouldn't like to abide in! (*Zing!*) One with a strange stone square or perhaps rectangle atop it, out of which black smoke pigtailed, then puffed, then streamed; then, weirdly, snowflakes of ash snowed down, then dancing fountains of blue, yellow, white, and bright pink sparks shot up. Which made one think this, thusly: "Hmm. Why is there a fire (what else could it be?) *inside* a house, an ostensible domicile? Where else might smoke come from but fire? *Ipso facto.* Q.E.D. Where there is smoke, there's fire. Someone said that, I believe. Who? I? Who knows? Logically, one wonders if there *are* people inside such an edifice—while it has a fire inside it? How could that be? And what sort of people? If on fire, the people inside, what needs must we have to do with them—surely fire will take care of them, lick them up, burn them, make quick work of them and spare us the work of slaying? But why, if people on fire, people not screaming in agony from being burnt alive *by* fire? All very odd. Another conundrum. If not on fire, then, perhaps they are fugitives. Fugitives plural. Warming themselves, also plural, somehow. While we, their conquerors, are here in the outside and quite frankly quite bitter cold, teeth-chatteringly so, blue of face and hand, freezing our balls off, the testicles, testes, that is, one's nards, the family jewels, sausage-and-eggs and what-you-will." [*Editor's note: Caius' confusion here can be attributed to the fact that fireplaces, hearths, etc. were unknown in Rome at the time; domiciles were warmed and lit by torches, either mounted or, in the best houses, held by slaves; a fire in the house was an unthinkable thing to your average Roman.*] I had a think about it. Thought I: "Hmmmm. What do here? What ought we do? Could be armed, they. Armed and dangerous, plus hungry and angry and toasty warm. Armed-hungry-angry-toasty warm combination not good. Esp. if armed to teeth. Esp. if teeth fanglike and chompy. Vicious. Bared. Even if nodose and sparse, said tooths. Have myself a big, big fear of being bitten, biters, people who use their teeth to their advantage and to your consequent disadvantage. As you know, as child I was bitten by a dog. And a snake. And a barracuda. And another dog. And a hyena. And a rat. And another snake. And a sea lion. And a horse (hence fear of all things equestrian). And a kangaroo. And a monkey. And a chimpanzee. And one of my childhood playfellows. And another one. And my own brother (a biter). And a Gila monster. And a parrot. And a...can't think now, but there was one more. It'll probably come to me in the middle of the night, it will, and the point is, well, I've been bitten quite a bit. Hahaha! Get it? Bitten...bit! Hahaha. Believe me, Lora, I have seen some very strange things, some very strange creatures, campaigning, in my day—some very odd birds. Plus customs. Real weird ones, many of them have. All right." So: "Not be hasty, let's," I says to myself as I think and think about how to deal with this situation of the maybe people in smoking building. "All right then," I says at last—decisive, authoritative, not mincing words like usual, but commanding, manly, captainish. Then I tells meself to take breath. Deep breath. Think. Make plan. Have plan. Plan involving Beefy, say. Send *him* in. If risk involved, have him take it. Serve him right. Get him back for all his rancid, brazen, decidedly smug beefing. Get him back and grandly. Make decision. Take action. Action involving Beefy *qua* platoon risk-taker designated. After having a think about it, squad leader *moi* (a.k.a. "The Decider") goes: "Here's the deal. Beef—you got one in you? A great big big one?" "Huh?" says he. "*You* know," I says. "Oh," he goes, shrugs, "I mean, I guess I could. I mean, sure." "Right," I says and points the way. "Marcellus, you listening to me, yeah? Listen here now: you go on and creep up to that thatched door—see that door, the thatched one?" Marcellus does. Nods. "Good," I says. "You creep up that thatched door, Beefy's right behind you, right?" Marcellus smirking, liking plan. "Right," Marcellus said. "You with me?" I says. "Right," say both. "All right, then. You creep up both—then, Marcellus, you poke it open—the door, that is—with a short, sharp kick, then Beef jumps forth, turns round, and quote-unquote fumigates the place with a blast from his ass. Got it?" "Um-hmm," both um-hmm. "Beefy beefs them out," Marcellus says. "Quite right," I says. Whispering, I continue: "Fuckers [again, pardon my language but war is Hades—we all know that]—if there are any in there, and I think there might well be some—will scramble and scurry *toute de suite* right the heck out of there once they get a whiff of old 'Below Aeolus' or whatever here. Then, as they're coughing and holding their hooters from the stench, we go in and slay them lickety-split, like. All right? And *then*, mind—well, just think of the story we'll have to tell Lt. Optio. Now: the plan I just told you—got it?" "Right," Beefy says. "Right," Marcellus says. "Right-right?" I says. "Right-right," they both say. "Good," I says. "Good-good," Beefy says. "Grand," I says. "Take some deep breaths, all right, Beef?" says I and I kinda puffs me chest out and waves me hands out like I'm splashing my face with water to illustrate regulated breathing—in, out, in, out, just so, like that. "Get some extra wind in ye. Got it?" "Fine," he says. "You sure?" "Fine. Grand," he says. "Let's do this!" I says. "Let's do *this!*" he says. "No, no, no," I says: "It's 'Let's *do* this!' You put the emphasis, the stress on the..." "Oh," Beefy goes. "Right. '*Let's* do *this!*'" he goes and just stands there. "Forget it," I says. Beat. Beat. More beats, with neither of them two knuckleheaded chuckleheads moving, getting going, getting a move on, creeping, etc. "Uh," I says and sighs and profoundly meaningfully, "ain't you forgetting somefink?" "Huh?" Beef says. "For Mercury's sake, start creeping— smartish!" "Oh," Beefy says. "Us? Now?" "Yes," says I, between gritted teeth. "Yes, yes, *yes*," says I. "Aye-aye. Sorry, sir," Beef wheezes inaccurately. Away they go, creeping, us crouching, watching—all ten. All was still. Very still. Too still. Then the wind hummed in the oscillating trees, making the leaves sough here, sough there, rustle, flutter, sigh. I don't know why but suddenly all seemed wrong, ominous. "Be careful!" I said a bit perhaps too volubly, cupping my hands round my mouth like a town crier, as they, the two buffoons, got halfway there, them scrambling slowly, deliberately zigzaggedly. I was a bit concerned for them, I must admit; I began to second-guess my plan. In retrospect, I'm sort of chiding myself for not trying to play the ventriloquist, or at least disguising my voice somehow, donning a Visigoth or South or Central Latvian accent or something. Because, well, let me tell you somefink, Lora: the damned inhabitants in that grassy-assed longhouse must've been of the educated ilk of indigenous longhouse inhabitants and spoken fairly good Latin or at least well-understood it on account of they must've overheard us (i.e. me) and were ready for us (well, for Beefy), 'cause soon as Marcellus swift-kicked the door open with a big old hypermelodramatic *bang!* and Beef stuck his big fat bum in to rip them a good one, some squat, smiling, motley-looking tooth-free churl with a hot poker like what you use for a roaring, midwinter courtyard fire dodges round all leprechaun-like and the blighter *in a flash* gets said hot poker (complete with one of them fleur-de-lis on the end of it, a *hook*, like; and I mean the thing was white hot and bright orange and sparkling red with diabolically hot heat—it must've come straight from lying or laying in the hottest-whitest coals)—the blighter, I say, points it and gets it, that nasty thing, right smack up Beefy's proffered bumhole, gets it up him good and deep, as he's bending over to "beef" one, "beef them out," as instructed. As suggested, I mean. What a cock-up! A recon gone wrong and no mistake. Unbelievable. And godsdammit if good old dear old windy Beeflicus just then didn't yelp like a thrice-fucked banshee and jump three feet off the ground, then do a hop, skip, and another jump like he was a qualifier for the what-d'ye-call-it event in the Olympics? The triple jump. Heading sort of diagonally off, obviously discombobulated, he was going "Ouch, ouch, oouch, eeuch," etc. And running holding with both hands his now-smoking bum. "Make for that lake, Beefy boy!" Marcellus shouted and pointed north, lakeways. "Jump in, cool your arse down!" said he. And *then* did not he, Beefy, yelp "Oh, good idea," and take off running like a bloody crazy madman toward the lake or lakelet or pond, excruciatingly bluer than blue as it was in the coolly placid afternoon. Here's a bit of regrettable ignominy, though: for I must admit we was all of us and verily trying very hard not to laugh (and failing 'cause by gods if it wasn't *the funniest thing I've ever seen*). Well, though, here's the sad and bad part: Beef didn't quite make it to the water, it being quite marshy all round the joint, there was a neighboring bed of quavering quicksand, crapulous green and yellow as anything, with twigs, leaves, fur hats, small bones, childrens' clothing, etc. floating on it. When we got up close and had a better gander, I was put in mind of the sawdust they use to tidy up vomitoria. A grotesque sight, in other words. Anyway, Beef being occupied running pell mell and yelping and holding that great fat giant arse of his like it were in a sling, he must've not noticed it, that fatal quickswamp, must've plashed plop *splat!* right into it, that wet trap of icky death. And the treacherously quicksandy bed, before we could get a rope to him or anything, try and fling him one of our red cloaks tied to another red cloak, became his last resting place, gods rest his obnoxiously flatulent soul. I feel a bit guilty on account of admittedly there *was* something of a pause between us hearing his piercing, desperate cries for assistance and us taking off dashing-sprinting madly after him. Well, maybe even more than a pause; more like a pause and another one, a very long one. I mean, eff me, but we (I in particular) just could *not* stop laughing. You ever tried legging it while you're giggling like crazy? Not easy. Before we all started wheeling after good old poor old unfortunate Beefboy, Marcellus for instance was on his ruddy knees and sort of salaaming, then holding his sides like a Jai-crying Hindu or German or Saxon had spiked or truncheoned or stabbed or arrowed him there, and sending skirling peals of bonkers laughter to the very skies. Lucretius—another of our party—was fairly crying, he was laughing so hard. And Claudius had to breathe into a big fat sack we were using for picking up spoils, he was hyperventilating so bad from mirth, delight. Gods, I wish you could've been there, Lor. It really was the funniest thing you've ever seen—or it would have been, had you seen it. I did, and it was. I'll always wonder if Beefy didn't try to blast his way out or something but the bubbles that bubbled and burbled and gurgled to the surface as we got there could've easily just come from his mouth, his last breaths on earth, poor sod. Or under it, in a sort of vibrating bayou, as the case may have been. Poor guy. Poor Beef. I can't believe that happened. I just can't believe it. And as I said, I feel terrible about it. He always did like a good larf, he did. Not as much as I do, of course. Does anyone like to yuck it up, laugh it up, and chuck around the old discus of hilarity more than I? I doubt it greatly: I'd like to meet the chap who's jollier, if he exists. I feel responsible: but you know, I'm not a bloody officer, he didn't *have* to obey me; he didn't *have* to go. It was no order or command—just an idea, just a wink and a nod. He and Marcellus as well could have said "No, fanx. Not doing that. Not creeping, kicking, beefing, etc." And he'd probably, gods willing, be alive today, gods rest his smelly soul. Here's a thought. Here's a bit of a philosophical quandary or conundrum: how interesting it is, how bizarre in fact, that we let ourselves off the proverbial hook whenever we can. How readily we find/make excuses for our faults and foibles. I'm convinced that humankind cannot bear very much reality, on the whole. I feel so low. How low, you ask or perhaps just wonder? This low: as though I should have been a pair of ragged claws, scuttling across the floors of silent seas. I feel all hollow. As though I am a hollow man. Honestly. That's how bad I feel. And yet, I'll live. I'll go on, washing in the morning and enjoying the sun, killing the enemy and wondering what's for tiffin, trying to think up original jokes and having a laugh with the chaps, writing to you each night by spluttering candlelight and sleeping and dreaming and snoring and farting. I'll continue to daydream and to think about myself, my life, what a wonder it is; myself and you and the kids. I'll make up more little tunes on my lute, and perhaps learn the flute. I'll look after my loot. Make sure the lock on my spoils chest is stuck on good and proper. I'll eat and drink and sometimes feast. I say! I'm not going to berate myself forever for this. Over this. I'm not going to feel guilty just because I'm pretty much a thoroughgoing knave here. I will say it again—humankind cannot bear, etc. Who of us can dwell for long on his mistakes? None of us. None. What do you think, Lora? Do you agree? It seems to me (for what it's worth) that we just can't take, as it were, the awful things we've done, how we've failed, come up short, choked, gooned, effed up, let down the side, the team, ourselves. Oh, well. The ridiculous and completely superfluous mission itself was an unalloyed failure anyway: zilch kills and no prisoners on mop-up detail. I had to fabricate (just between you and me, you know—I hope the censors don't catch this—Hail, censors!) one kill and two mortally wounded escapees. Told them we lopped off one arm and one hand but they were swift of foot and made it to the dark and thickly misty woods and disappeared before we could catch up with them. I mean, mess-ups like this one was is why we have officers and non-coms, not guys (*grunts*) like me, in charge. I'm no brilliant military strategist, no battle tactitian (sp?) à la the frowning generals and the all-but-invisible higher higher-ups who, likely enough, went as legacies to some of the top military schools and have campaigning in their respective brassy bloods all the way back to Romulus, no less. On said mop-up ops and fall-back encounters, we just sort of wing it, *sans* supervision, and...well...you see what sometimes eventuates: guys like Beefy sink in quicksand and die, die, die. As you know, I'm just a regular guy (an amiable guy, wouldn't you say?) With regular ambitions and regular stools and regular adherences to regular regulations and regular hopes and regular dreams and an irregular helmet and...and an equally singularly irregular sense of humor and a regular mind and a regular yen to write long letters. The kinda guy who just wants to get a few kills now and then and get back to his spectacular, loving, sexy minx of a wife and kids and start a new life, kick back a bit, get his kilt/kit off, put down his blunted sword and snapped-in-half lance and seek out/find a new career in original comedic onstage entertainment. I ask you: is that too much to ask? Too much to expect of a long (or short, depending) life. What a joke it all seems. But this— today—was the wrong kind of joke. Nobody's laughing now. Nobody's amused or even grinning. As I mentioned, 'twas a mess and shambles, though not all my fault, as I've tried to show—we were all of us foxed, not just me alone. To crown all, the crafty, diabolical longhouse denizens must've seized the op to make a dash for it while we all stood round the quicksand (or mud) with our thumbs up our bums or fingers in our gobs, horrified and out of breath: for when we went back to the domicile and just barged in with swords out, intending vengeance of the most severe kind and meaning to punish them in the *penetralia* "with extreme prejudice," as they say, and there was nobody there, no toothless poker fellow, nobody. Not a soul. Vanished, they was (had?). Sprites of some sort might they have been, Lora. Strange. Now Beefy's dead and gone to the happy hallowed Fields of E, I wonder who will be my new kipfellow? How was your day, by the way? What a story, eh? What a tale. And all of it mostly true. Looking forward to hearing from you, and as always I remain

Your Caius Aquilla

P.S. Too tired to write a post scriptum—after the enormity and the shock of today. Beddy-bye for me, my love. Sweet dreams. Mine, I reckon, will be haunted by a ghost of someone. Someone called "Beefy."

P.P.S. Well, not too too tired, I suppose. Oh! Forgot to mention: the other night I had to thwack a rat. Middle of the night I hear this nibble-nibbling and sort of scratchy-scratching sound and guess what? Yes, you guessed right. A rat. In our tent. That's right. Enormous. I had to thwack him. Thwack him good. And I did. Then tossed him out the tent flap. End of story. End of rat's story, anyway. Nasty things, rats. Horrid.

XX FEBRUARIUS

Dear Friend:

Hail and forgive me as I haven't had time to write for a week now. Instead of heading south as I'd hoped we've gone southeast, sorry to report. The old gold eagles bob, the pennants flap snappishly, the officers' horses' arses boom-chicka-boom in the tall cold blue sky as we march on and on, following the scudding pink-and-white or just plain pink puffy clouds. The music of clinking armor serenades us cacophonously to the tattoo of hundreds of lock-step marching feet, on and on. Lieutenant Optio told us, at dinner, whispering conspiratorially, that the higher higher-ups in Rome have sent a long letter (in short order) to the generals. It goes pleading for one more maneuver before we get to hie us home. I wonder why they ever bother asking. They could just write "More kills and crucifixions, if you please, on your way back to The Eternal City" and have done with it. Why all these formalities, these gratuitous requests? They could just say: "Well, long as you're heading this way, why not subdue yet another race of inferiors? Doesn't that sound nice? Doesn't it sound a bit of all right, a bit of fun, lads?" Excrement! I'm so dismayed. I thought we were done here. Oh well. Sorry, love. Try not to be too sad yourself. They say it'll only be a matter of a month or two but who knows. We're all of us dead tired and homesick and in need of a meal that's not been slopped forth from a ladle. How I would love to be with you, just you, somewhere—near the gray-blue sea, say. Us (we?) two. Or picnicking up the Palatine Hill or watching some opulent pageantry or other—gladiators or orators nattering on about some such grand thing or other. How boring war is sometimes. How tired I am always. Tired, tired, tired. It never thought it possible to be this ridiculously exhausted. I'm fighting sleep as I slog along. It's almost as bad as sparring with Spartans. I'm not the only one who's knackered on his feet. Good old Marcellus started talking as he was walking and suddenly it struck me that he was bloody *sleepwalking*. Sleepmarching, I mean—to coin a phrase. How's that even possible? Maybe he was having us all on and playing the facetious somnambulist, but I don't think so: 'twas too convincing for him to be shamming. I need a nap badly.

I've never been more fagged out in me entire life, I tell you. And the aches and pains? Merciless and relentless. Indefatigably indefatigable. It's like a carnival of them or something: I've got iridescent blisters on both hands, niggling little cuts all over the shop, sore thighs and lower back, and my left knee's killing me, throbbing like anything from when I twisted it and badly two frays ago or so. Here's how it happened: cutting and thrusting and fighting *mano-a-mano,* Joc turned to me and said something like "Hey, Caius—watch me take this stupid barb's leg off with a simple parry!" And as I spun round to watch him I felt this popping sound go *snap!* in the deepest part of my meniscus. Soon as one particular hurt's all but forgotten, another crops up. I've had a severe, unstinting, beastly toothache that's been acting up of late (remind me to go see the toothpuller soon as I come home, Lora; I keep putting it off). No sooner do I go "Ouch!" and grip my right cheek than does my elbow start thrumming unceasingly and amazingly, alarmingly painfully from when I banged it the other day on a dried-up tree stump as I was stretching, doing some pre-fray calisthenics. And it all goes round and round. At the end of any given attack-day, it's like I'm doing a parody of Grecian stretching exercises. You know the ones where you touch one part of your body, stretch, lunge, crouch, get up, touch another part, stretch, lunge, etc.? I believe they call them "burpees." On account of...well, you know. It's like that. That bad. Like this one time when Marcellus, having lost his gourd-canteen somehow, got a full body cramp and had to knead madly with all his might his cramping thigh muscle, then his chest, then his calves, then back to his chest, then his stomach, then his buttocks, etc.—just ridiculous. There are few things funnier. I need a proper massage so badly but those are only given gratis to the centurions and the officers and of course the generals and the overlordly higher higher-ups. We, the grunts, the worker bees (unfortunate term) who really need a good hard old fashioned Oriental rub-down/pounding after work, have to pay out and dearly a big part of our paltry salaries for those sorts of luxuries and amenities, and as you know I'm trying to be as cheese-paring if not frugal as I can so as to buy our precious/sweet kids something nice for their birthdays this year. I can hardly keep my poor old weary eyes on the old papyrus right now, Lora. I must add that I've been going rather *berserk* during the skirmishes. (I've been meaning to find an op to use that word—it's one I learned from a cove who fought some mercenary Norsemen a couple of years ago. Isn't it neat? Isn't it funny-sounding? I love it. The fellow said it meant "to go crazy during battle, plus raping and pillaging." Sounds rather a good time, doesn't it? I hope we get to meet some of these Norsemen. Then kill them, of course. They sound like rather good chaps, I daresay.) Well then: I really really really really really need to go lay me down now, go night-night, hit the sack, hit the hay, flog myself to sleep (thinking of you, your mouth, of you on top, then me astraddle, then of taking you from behind) and let the Sandman have his way with me and all of that. But here I am, up and diligently-faithfully writing, writing, writing, because, dear friend, I love you so and miss you so. My little yellow tallow candle's spluttering and guttering: 'tis surely a sign I ought to sign off and try and get XL winks. One thing before I leave off: a wee request? Would you be so kind as to, in your next, recount some happier happy times of ours—our wedding, say? Or the honeymoon? Or the time for jollity's sake good old Joculator let loose into our courtyard just the cutest baby crocodile. Remember that? It was shortly after we were newly married and came back from said halcyon honeymoon. That was a complete scream, just hilarious; he really is a master of humor, a true and veritable jokesmith, practical and otherwise. Ah, gods, I wish I could kiss you right now and cup and pat and palpate your nice fat white thighs and svelte waist and fine hips and great and succulent-sweet breasts and esp. your sweet, sweet and not-too-big Lorabum. And so to bed. (Cot, *id est.*) Exhaustedly,

Your Caius Aquilla

P.S. Zzzzzzzzzz... Please let me know, by the by, if my letters are getting through: this makes at least three I've sent that I can only hope have reached your soft white lovely clouds of hands.

II APRILLUS

Dear Friend:

Hail! All's well here at home in halcyon Rome, dear friend, & I am indeed in receipt of your last—your last three, actually; the post's been particularly good, along with the superbly & surprisingly clement, favonian weather. It's sun, sun, sun for us the past few days; everything spangles & sparkles colorfully in a sky that's by turns blue & mellow oatmeal & mild gold all over our fair city. The sunshine's only too welcome after so many desperately depressing cloudy days in a ragged row. There's a nice breeze, too. & furthermore they say the grain harvest was plentiful enough last year that, should it happen not to be so very great this year, the plebs won't starve. Hence we can all relax & assume there won't be much grousing & unrest or—gods forbid!—any sort of incipient uprising amongst the undesirables, the hoi polloi, the riff-raff, losers, commoners, et alia. I miss you heaps, you know. I do so very hate to go harping (pun!) on my own burdens, but you must know that it's really quite hard on me, Caius Aquilla, having you away again & for who knows how long. Nevertheless, well I understand that of course the empire & the glory of Rome come first; & we poor thumb-twiddling, deep-sighing, bored-silly, understanding, & goodly wives must wait & wonder & keep ourselves busy with children & trifles & try not to fret & sport-eat & wring our hands right off our wrists with obsessive worry! *You* aren't to worry, by the by. Rest assured we're all of us safe & sound, snug & not inordinately unhappy. Spring has sprung: fresh pink flowers wink in profusion from the bowls on our tables, carnations, roses, lilies; birds dance in the air and work their happy melodies; human voices call to each other from beyond the walls of our yard, voices merry & jovial, twinkling with chummy energy & liveliness & enterprise. I haven't all that much to report, sooth to say, sorry to say, save the humdrum fact that I'm getting along pretty well with my music lessons, learning new tunes & pleasing runs & little riffs & scales & ditties all the time; becoming more & more fond of my instrument the better I get to know it. Let's see: what else? Perhaps on account of the erstwhile dreadfully overcast stretch of weather, Aurelian's had a very bad cold, very rheumy, sniffly, listless, mopey, enervated, cranky, whingeing, helpless, crusty. He's been kept home from *ludus*, which is of course sheer torture for him as he loves his ancient doddering schoolmaster Master Seneca Maximus & he's rather terribly if not frightfully popular with the four other kids he goes to school with. He's such a bright star, such a tyro senator already. As you know, Seneca Maximus doesn't take every *puer* who just applies: he's frightfully selective & the Socratic interview was grueling. It didn't help that you weren't here to go through it with me. SM likes a family that presents a unified front, where both parents are there, present, helping with the homework & not off subduing inferior, subpar peoples: I don't mean to remonstrate with you here so harshly, Caius Aquilla, but you have no idea how much homework—piles of it, really & truly—Aurelian ports in each night. Though no doubt Master Seneca's worth it—every denarius, every silver or copper coin that we/I cross his aged palm with. There's a waiting-scroll to get in like you wouldn't believe—everyone wants him, everyone adores him. Drusilla's mollycoddled kids didn't even get an audition. I don't mean that cattily, but still—pretty grand, wouldn't you say, that we got an epistle of acceptance so quickly. I had one of the servants paste it up on the larder with some glue made from coconut milk and the sinews of various expired horses, Jews & Christians & barbarians. They melt them down in cauldrons in foundries on the edge of the city, I believe. Most interesting. You never know what inventions our Roman engineers will mastermind next! You know, we should be very proud of him, Aurelian, & of ourselves (you *in absentia*), for holding out for the best fit, schoolwise. Truth be told, it's the best in the city & hence the entire world. It's not hubris. And of course I hate to brag but I have to: Aurelian's so cute & so smart & funny & sweet & witty & adorable. Such a fiery little noble already, the way he thrashes the cats & rides our giant tortoise round the terrace, whipping it "hut-hut!" & all that rot. How his eyes sparkle when I thrash the servants for one of their many quotidian stupidities. How I love to see him play! So free, such a blithe little spirit. Let's see. What else? Oh! Here's story you'll surely appreciate: the other night, a darkling new moon one, Aurelian looked up in the starry sky & pointed & said: "Look, mummy. Mummy, look! The moon's not open. The moon is closed." I nearly started weeping with pride & sentimental sentimentality. Such a bright, clever little boy that boy of yours. I mean, how poetic was that?! "The moon's closed." Surely, if he doesn't become a senator or centurion he'll be an epic *vates* & write great books to rival Homer's, big heavy ones, as impossible to lift as they would be to comprehend. Perhaps he'll oversee a colony one day, become a magistrate or potentate or governor, be recognized by some great Caesar-or-Senate-to-come. I can envision him expatiating on some obscure law or sitting in state on a great & imposing chair, officiating at a tribunal, having commanded someone's hands be lopped off or banishing someone else to some faraway island or wilderness. Proud I am of him no end! I let him have an entire stalk of sugar cane for that one, that quip about the moon, & a handful of candied gooseberry & lime jellies, plus a dish of strawberries & cream, then some watered wine—a glass or two only, elderberry, I think it was. He just can't stop with the adorable adorability. Pretty near every day he comes up with something that makes me tingle with joy. You won't remember this one either, 'cause you weren't there: when he was five Aurelian was playing with one of those wooden toy racing chariots you gave him—the painted purple & white & gold ones. I spotted him turning it into a war chariot, zooming it round & round on the freshly scrubbed marble floors, pantomiming having the toy driver with his splendid red cape & pristine tunic & heigh-ho sword raised high going running over & smiting every last one of his painted Jews & Samaritans & Goths & craven Thracians. Such a look of concentration on his fierce face there was. & I said with a broad-big maternal smile on *my* lovely, loving face: "Aurelian-darling—why do you like chariots so much?" & he just looked up preciously & shrugged his bold little shoulders & said: "Because they get me where I need to go." Isn't that incredible? Utterly wonderful. So sweet & cute he is—I could eat him alive for breakfast, turn temporary cannibal & have him roasted then glazed with raspberry sauce & lap him up with a spoon, mop up every bit of him with a round of good bread from the heart of the country. He'd be delicious! Hahaha! Anyway, Caius, don't be upset about the treats he's been given, if you don't mind: every sweet he eats, each goblet he downs is one less for me, you'll be pleased to be reminded. Ha! I know I have an insatiable sweet tooth—& a hollow leg to boot. You know how I struggle with it. You know my demons. It's the bane of my existence, this weakness, this perpetual craving for succulent savory sweets—a sugarcoated Achilles heel, if you will. You needn't remind me of it every third epistle, descant upon it at length as though it were a pet subject with you, a hobby horse, etc. Just a nudge, so to speak, from your I-know-you-consider-me-flumpity bride. So there. Enough. What else? Where was I? Oh! Sorry to mention horses: I know how you—speaking of demons—fear them, or at least do all you can to avoid them. Nevertheless, *do* stop telling me what to do, what to eat, not to drink, etc. How tiresome that is—don't you see? Thank you very much, I can manage my diet on my own. I don't need your input; but I do need your support. Got it? Good. What *to* report, now I've chided you good & proper you for your unseemly officiousness? Think I'll pour out an enormous tumbler of wine right now—in your honor & just to spite you, just for the Hades of it! Drink deep from some beaker of the warm south. Watch the beading bubbles wink at me from my favorite goblet, hoist a toast to you so very far away & proceed to opiate myself with liquid happiness. Hear that sound from all this distance, husband? *Splishy-splashy!* It's the sound of me pouring forth. Enough! I'm sick of this chastisement, & of all the allusions to my problems. I thought you were on my side. & quite frankly I'm a bit mystified as to where this rather rum over-concern for me's coming from! I sort of assumed when we married that you were something of a lipophile. That's, in part, why we made such a pretty pair. Am I wrong? Right? & get this, mister: I *like* the way I look, all right? Whether it's in looking glass or bath or basin I *like* what I see when my everyone-says-lovely visage in reflection gazes fondly back at me. Understood? Got it? Fine. Sorted. Now leave it out, won't you? I've had about enough & that's that & no mistake. Now let's see: what else can I tell you? Julia's growing like a weed: you wouldn't recognize her. The other day she asked me if we could put one of the monkeys on one of the donkeys so it could have a nice "wide awound the yard." Where on terra firma'd she get an idea like that, I shouldn't wonder? That a monkey could ride a donkey, around the yard, no less? You've never taken her to the *circus* or the *races* without my knowing, have you? Of course not. I hope not. I bet you have, though. You're *very* bad, Caius Aquilla: you spoil them. & spoil me. Those lovely flowers you had your niece send me? Those *were* from you, right? I hope so! Otherwise... Oh, Caius. Dear husband, dear friend, I hope you know I do love you so. & speaking of spoils & spoiling: no monkeys, when you return this time, all right? No monkeys & no necklaces made from the teeth of eww-y barbarian children. What next—a shrunken head? "Hello, love," I can just hear you saying, smirking, biting your lip the way you do when you're being coy & crafty & have a surprise for me: "Brought you somefink: 'ere you go, love—the head of barbarian, shrunken! Innit great?! Innit terrific?!" No thanks. Gross! Oh, how I wish you were here— without said head, of course. I'm really horny right now; think I'll have a lie down for a bit while the children are napping & think of you while I...

you know. I mean, you're not the only one with needs of that kind, yeah; I find that I get hornier & hornier as I get older, oddly enough... Okay. I'm back. Where was I? Oh, off to fantasyland, thinking how I've just been very exceedingly randy & dying to be touched & kissed & ravished—taken from behind. I wanted you so bad a minute or so ago; I hate this. Today I do, I reckon. Some days are easier to bear than others. Some days I don't even think about you even for an instant, I'm so busy practicing the harp, reading poems, exercising (yeah, right!) in our compound yard, bossing & beating the servant slaves, reading Roman histories, snacking, organizing meals, & watching the darling children play & do their respective lessons. I do so like to spectate while Aurelian's giving old Master Seneca a run for his money, sword fighting-wise, heaving his little toy wooden cutlass (despite the fact that old Seneca has the reflexes of a bloody just-fed house cat or common garden lizard doing push-ups in the sun): I can just picture Aurelian, when he's older, of course, running right through the breastplate or brisket some bastard of a Jute or a refractory Mesopotamian, some jai-crying, blue-painted Hindu, acquitting himself honorably on the glorious field of battle & killing all manner of foes, enduring war's horrors & becoming quite the renowned warrior & bloodthirsty slaughter king! How lovely that would be, to see him laureled something, empurpled with glory, deigning to nod to a multitude of fawning sycophants & admirers & women throwing themselves at him! Anyway, please come home safe. & soon. Dear darling brave sweet silly Caius Aquilla-husband! How I too long for the warmth of your arms. But not too warm, please. I pray the gods every night on my very knees to bring you back in one piece to me & the kiddies. Anyway, one more thing about spoils & all that might make you smile: these days I can make my own human tooth necklaces, seeing as Aurelian keeps losing them like your slutty sisters their virginity! (Just joking—they're five of the nicest whores I know, the trollops!) Two of his fell out this week! I sacrificed a rabbit & a turkey & an ostrich to Mercury to speed his good growth, dentalwise. Really, though, Caius, I must say that even though they're growing apace both young monkeys are still far too little for such sights as are customarily displayed in the Circus Maximus. You mustn't take them there again, all right? Promise me you won't do that again. That was most naughty of you. Alas! Next thing you know you'll be sneaking them off to a battlefield to watch you at work! Not good. I understand they need breaks from time to time from their breakneck schedules, but still. I do wonder if we have them doing too much these days, with their every waking moment regimented & accounted for. Aurelian breaks his lavish fast from eight till ten-thirty, then, after a quick nap, Master Seneca from eleven to noon; recess & gallivanting about the yard for an hour; more tutoring; swordplay; then on Tuesdays, Thursdays & Saturdays he has Archery; and on Wednesdays & Fridays Legion Scouts; Sunday afternoon is Latin Book Club; & Mondays he has Junior Senate Debating & Diplomacy. Precious Julia likewise doesn't seem to have a minute to herself (aside from meals & playtime & nap-times) to save her life! Drama With Dolls all morning; Reading & Writing with her nanny; a Play Date in the afternoon (if we can orchestrate it); & Playing Dress Up & Choosing Jewelry every weekend afternoon. I myself am exhausted just thinking about the chalkboard in the foyer that I continually have to consult in order to know where the poor ambitious dears are in the course of sun-up to sundown. Poor dears. I know you think I'm overprotective but Rome's changing so rapidly these days & kids grow up too fast, methinks, even the ones that are cossetted & doted upon overmuch, as ours incontrovertibly are. What little innocence they've got left I'd like to preserve for as long as I can, if I may. As a matter of fact t'other day I had to shield both their precious little pairs of eyes as, past the usual beastly beggars, ghastly cripples, hideous moneylenders, & absolutely appalling ancients as through rivulets of muck, we charioted it over to Drusilla's for a luncheon-time playdate. A horrible Persian merchant, all beetling brows and insane flaring nostrils and fish-eyed, was slave-driving his slave through the traffic-jammed marketplace with a great brown-and-white candy-striped bullwhip. Some giant of a mutant African bastard, the slave was, with the saddest, most dreamy-dreary big light brown eyes you've ever seen. Blood sprinkled my best pale orange frock, I tell you. Did it not! Absolutely appalling. It looked, my frock, like some portrait painter's drop cloth or a mosaic done up by a madman. The blood from the guy's brawny black back splashed right at us, & some of it freckled my fucking face, if you can believe *that*. Unbelievable. Julia said: "Mummy, you've have got [sic] wittle red butterflies on your face! They're pretty, mummy. You're pretty too!" & laughed & laughed. A sweetish moment, surely, but what's the city coming to, anyway? Absolutely incredible & unconscionable, if you ask me. I couldn't believe it, what I saw. "But seriously, what is that on 'ur' cloak & face, mummy?" Julia said, the sweet little innocent dear. Mind you, I was quite shocked. Had to think on my feet & very fast & no mistake. "That?" I said. "Oh, nothing, love. Just pomegranate juice." "That man who just got whipped bled *pomegranate* juice?" Aurelian said & screwed up his lovely little peachy-creamy face. "That can't be right, mummy," he said all stout & sitting up straight. I didn't know *what* to reply, I swear to gods. Telling ya. The child just busted me completely. Just proves: you should never ever lie to kids. But what? What should I have told him? *Then Julia asked if she could taste it*, see what pomegranate tasted like—she actually wanted to lick it, my garment! Appalling, I'm telling you. Both of them, our progeny, strawberry-sweet & innocent as the *diem* is long. As our driver sheared off, as per my stentorian orders, me tongue-lashing him to bloody get the demons the Hades out of there, I had to distract them (Aurelian & Julia) with a positively ridiculously phony story about a very pretty little lonely pony who belongs to the Legion & who gets lost after a nasty & astonishingly bloody skirmish, then finds his way home by asking some helpful-friendly goats & a brave little roadrunner to point out the way—a story, I'll have you know, they saw right through from the get-go. You could tell that the entire time I was making this ludic dreck up they were only thinking about what they'd horripilatingly seen through my splayed & fumbling & dancing fingers. I mean, the savage look on the master's face as he wound up & let fly was something *I* should never like to see the likes of again, let alone allow the kiddies to peep at, despite the fact that I must admit I might have stopped & gawked a bit were the kids not there: 'twas the sort of scene that's so disturbing, so fascinating, really, that one can't tear one's eyes away. Sooner tear them out than away, really. Such an unimaginably grotesque display of ire & unmitigated thrilling savagery. People are just beasts sometimes. *Beasts,* I tell you. Brutes. I *hate* them. I hate that I'm flabbergasted at what they, these so-called humans, can do. & *you* tell *me* if you don't think civilization's just going straight to the dogs. I wonder what the poor slave did to warrant such a ruthless thrashing? Deserved it, probably. But have a bit of decency & whip him in your own home, not in public, won't you, tough guy? I'm no great supporter of or even sympathizer to the philosophies of master Xeno (isn't he the infamous xenophobe: *so* hard to keep all these egghead Greeks straight; & xenophobia's kind of antithetical to our mission to Romanize the known world, no?), but some of these godsdamned arrivistes *are* beasts, I tell you. Sorry to keep repeating that term but. Oh! Speaking of which—gosh, I *do* have something to fill you in on, some news. Not good news, though. I don't know how to tell you this, Caius, so I'm just going to go ahead & just spit it out, just say it or write it, rather. Fido, your favorite old hound dog, is unfortunately dead. Apparently, Aurelian went to pet him this morning & have him chase a ball made of yellow wool & when he found him lying on his side on the cold bare kitchen floor he patted him (the mutt, the hound) a few times, he said, then thumped him *thwack!* a few times real good, he said; & then the poor sweet innocent dear boy came a-running, yelling: "Mummy, mummy, Fido won't wake up! Fido won't wake up! Fido won't wake up! There's something wrong with him, mummy! Fido won't wake up! What's wrong with him, mummy?! What's wrong?!" I went with him to see what the deal was & sure enough: dead as a doornail, sure as the world is flat. As Aurelian wept & wept & lay on top of the maculate, mangy old cur, embracing him heartbreakingly, his pretty little head nestled in the dead dog's neck fur, Julia chanted "Fiwdo dead, Fiwdo dwead, he's dwead, he's dwead, he's dwead!" She was jumping up & down corybantically & crying like a mad thing. You know—that little springy thing she does when she's upset. Strange thing: most people "jump for joy," right? Curious girl. I don't know where she got that from: neither you nor I act like that. We aren't "jumpy"! Even though she does indeed pogo up & down sometimes when she's excited in a good way. Perhaps it's only a phase or something. Anyway: "He *can't* be dead, mummy!" Aurelian sobbed & sobbed, looking up at me with *the* most pitiful look in his beautiful eyes; "Just yesterday he was fine! He kilt [sic] a big fat rat only two days ago, & I saw him chased [sic] & almost catched [sic] a mean old orange tabby just yesterday afternoon!" Chased! Ha! More like waddled after for two limpy steps, then lie a-down again, poor old hobbling—now deceased—thing. Nevertheless, they're both so cute I can't stand it sometimes. At IV and VII I think we have two of *the* most adorable little fuckers in all The Eternal City, don't you? & beautiful. Incomparably so. Everyone remarks upon it, their beauty. Don't you think they are—beautiful? Much more bonny than Drusilla's brats, certainly. I imagine Julia will grow to be a great beauty, in fact, & have many, many lovers and suitors, & perhaps be a famous courtesan or concubine. & Aurelian a right devil of a lady killer, smiting them left & right, ambidextrously, as it were. Anyway, sorry about good old Fi. He was faithful as his name & is now well out of it, this vast, expansive vale of tears we call life. The way at the end he hobbled when tossed a scrap of cow or a bit of boiled chicken or squab was just so sad to see, don't you think? (Oh what do you know, husband? I don't mean to henpeck but you're never here, you bastard.) Anyway, these past few months or so the children teased him (Fido) relentlessly: they'd dangle bits of their dinner at him, then pop them into their own gluttonous gobs; or the cats or birds would get the few measly scraps flung at him, make away with them (the scraps) before he could even get a shirt on, poor old cur, poor old canine smellfeast. Come to think of it, you ought to count yourself bloody lucky you *didn't* have to see your dear old pet dog dragging his bare bleeding old dead arse about the house these past few months. War's good for some

things, is it not? Cold comfort, I know, but still. I miss you. You know I
am with you whithersoever you roam...from Rome. Ha! Good one, huh?
Just like I know I'm not the only comedian in the family. I mean, you're
not the only funny one. Got distracted there for a sec as I thought I heard
someone call my name... Back in a jiffy... Okay, where was I? Oh, that
was neighbor Marius, coming over to say hello & "May I have a word?"'&
all of that fulsome & I daresay quite oleaginous stuff & nonsense &—
interestingly enough—to borrow a cup of honey if he might, etc. What
an absolutely bizarre request! I don't know if I've ever encountered the
like of it—borrowing something from a neighbor. Sooner ask to squat
over one of our chamber pots! Quite remarkable, really. Perhaps he's been
day-drinking (or what I like to just call 'drinking')! Dunno why he doesn't
have one of his servants toddle off to market for it. He's only lonely, I
suppose. Wants a wee chat. I could tell he'd have loved to stay for a quaff
of wine, a bit of "the grape" & a nice round of country bread, some
actual grapes, & a bit of fresh-made cheese & sweet young figs & ripe
mangos & candied almonds & plump & juicy strawberries & cream. (I
must be feeling peckish to write that out so lustily.) I will say one thing
re: Marius: it must be enormously difficult to lose one's spouse at twenty-
six, in the prime of life, don't you know. I shouldn't like to lose you, dear
friend, at any age. Funny—he's only two years younger than me and two
years older than you. Such a nice fellow, though, don't you think—affable
& stuff? & pretty amusing, pretty funny, too, despite his sugar-cane smiles
& honeyed words & verbal disabilities or handicaps or anomalies or
peccadilloes or whatever the vogue term is nowadays. What a strange
man! Very strange, actually. I don't know that I've ever met anyone like
him. "I'll pay you back in s-s-spades," he says brightly. "D-d-d-double, I
will. Sometime next m-m-month." With a frank wink he told me he's
thinking of taking up beekeeping! "Oh, joy," I tells him, "what a splendid
thing to have—a keeper of countless angry, dangerous, swarming, stinging
insects for a neighbor! You don't half know how to reassure a girl," I says.
He laughed at that one & pinched my bum & made a sound like buzzing.

The liberties you Roman men take sometimes! The absolute effrontery! No respect for the proprieties. You're all incorrigible. Plus unflappable. He's only lonely, I suppose. My most murderous glares are met with obstinate, importunate glances. I reckon he was only joking, coming on to me in that fashion. I sure do hope so. "Ca-Ca-Ca-Caius about?" he asks, twinkles in's eyes, things coming to a pretty pass between us, I should warrant. La, don't he full well know you're still away campaigning? "No?" says he with an even more horrid, knowing wink this time. He's a rare one for winking, the smarmy goon. "Why d-d-dontcha c-c-come over & take a d-d-d-draught with me one of these n-n-n-nights if you get to fidgeting," he says. "Fidgeting?" says I, all mortified astonishment, & he hems & haws a tad bit & stammers (or is his a stutter—I never know the difference, & when I look it up, the difference between a stammer & a stutter, I never remember it; it's like the term *a priori*—I can never recall what that signifies, despite the fact that I've researched it an hundred & five times at the least, honor bright, I tell you) further: "Y-y-*you* know—la-la-la-lonesome like; must be hard having your ma-ma-man a-wa-wa-way a-warring all the t-t-time, & you a ra-ra-ra..." "You mystify me, sir, but go on, then," I says, "spit it out, do." "Radiant la-la-lass, no less. Ra-ra-ravishing, also," he says. "Well, that's a routine compliment but I shall let it pass. Though you do lay it on with a trowel, as I'm a person! La! & speaking of *passes*, he'll—my *husband*, that is—know who to *thank* & thank you *very* much," I tells him over my shoulder & turns on my heel, meaning you'll have him to thank if anything, you know, happens between us, me & him, if you want me to spell it out for you, Caius. I've just gone & done so. "Sau-*cy!*" says sassy neighbor Marius & full-on palms me on the rump this time. Then, mind you, he runs after & takes my hand, turns me round like someone on a stage somewhere, some poxy actor type. The nerve of the zealous fellow! "Marius, what are you—what do you think you are—doing?" I said. Stares he, unnervingly, straight into my lovely, big, & beautiful (everybody says so) pale gray & sometimes hazel blue eyes, & his indeterminate-colored ones go all soft & sorry-soppy: "I can't help it,

Lora," he says. "It's been a very trying time, you know. You have the most beautiful g-g-gray eyes." Well, the last sentence I fabricated; he didn't say that, exactly, but by Argus he sure should have. Or something like that. Men always say too much—or too little. They flower it up—or leave an abundance of weeds. There's no in between, it seems. Demurely, I told him I understood, & bowed my head most *faux*-piously. I'm such a horrible coquette! Such acting—on my part as well! & from one who has little patience with anything thespianish. I can't believe the tricks I pull & get away with sometimes. Roman men, despite being the best in the world, are not always the brightest or the most gentlemanly-chivalrous, as I'm a person. A bunch of decadent ninnies they/you all are—when it comes to the unfixed rituals of courtship & seduction. Then I said—bless his little imbecile heart & ridiculous handicap—that I sincerely hoped things'd get better for him before too many more months went by, blah, blah, blah. I found I actually meant it! What a little fool I was being. La! Where in the world could such genuine tenderness come from? His eyes glow with almost tears & his risible muckle mouth quavers like a sea anemone does when you tickle it or poke it viciously with a wet stick or branch. Then, all mild & stuff, he goes: "I th-th-th-th..." "Thank you?" I says. "Y-y-yes," says he & goes on: "I thank you. Listen, th-th-though, L-L-Lora: you know how I've just t-t-toldja about the b-b-b-bees?" "Yes," I said, falling right straight into his trap. "& what of it?" says I, all haughty-like & I know not what. "I have about zero interest in bees, Marius," says I. He says: "Well now I'll t-t-t-teachja 'bout the *birds*, as well, I will! You come over one n-night & s-s-see, pretty m-m-missus. You always smell so n-n-nice, you know—what's that you're w-w-w...you've got on? Is it *eau du la-la-lavender*?" "No, I don't think so," I said. "Well, whatever it is—even were it sewer water or b-b-b-bilge—you *look* lovely as well. You're am-am-amazingly pretty, you know. I've always th-th-thought that. I've always had a th-th-thing for r-r-redheads, & you're the p-p-prettiest one I think I've ever s-s-seen." "Whatever do you *mean*, sirrah?" says I. "Come, come, Lora," says he, "no need to be kittenish about this!

I think you kn-kn-know ex-ex-precisely what I am driving at here! Surely you d-d do, madame." Goodness gracious, Caius Aquilla, I hope for the life of me it's all in good fun & egregious he's only fooling, only flirting. If he's not…well, the cheek of the fellow, pawing me like that outrageously & coming on to me so! I've never seen anyone so b-b-brazen. Cups my ass, flatters me flagitiously, propositions me, invites me over… Who's he think he is—Zeus or something? & me Leda & he The Swan in the old myth? He's only a lawyer, after all. Nothing special. Nothing to write home about, crow about. Swing a dead Egyptian cat & hit five & a half of them on any no-name street in this great town, yet they all think unquestionably that they're gods's gift to humanity, lawmen do. Damme if they don't. Godsdamned silvertongues! The pompous hubris of these guys, sometimes. I mean, really. If he really does mean business & is trying in earnest to seduce me, get in my tunic & have his way with me & fuck me silly sideways, soon as you get home I'm sure you'll show him "what for," thrash his stuttering-stammering ass as sure as Indivia's the goddess of jealousy. "I'm a happily married woman, Marius," I tells him, hand on one sassy, jutting hip, accompanied by a pert little moue—one of my best moues, actually, one I haul out only when serious business is meant, & afoot, & it's absolutely necessary to put a randy & frightfully forward man in his place & drive him mad with thwarted desire, inflame that desire, stoke it, feed it more & more kindling, fan it, then douse it, drench it with water or dash flour upon it with both fists full. Haha, I laugh. Ha. Ha. *Ha.* I daresay you've seen it—that champion look—more than a few times, you have. Works like a charm: man's in the proverbial palm of your etc. "Well, if you *say* so," he poutily & mock-bashfully & coyly says & gives us a rather meaning look. "I say," I says, "*do* stop playing the fool, won't you? It's most un-neighborly & most unbecoming. I'm not just… those aren't just empty words…" "It's just…" says he & pauses pregnantly. "What?!" says I (Damn him!). "Oh, nowt." "What?!" says I again. "I shouldn't say!" says he & turns away all mock-demure, like a schoolgirl whose nipples have hardened unaccountably. "Tell me!" I queen it. Sighs he again for the hundredth time prodigiously & he looks up at the sky & says: "Nothing, Lora. Nothing, nothing, nothing, nothing. It doesn't matter. Have it your own way, I su-su-ppose." Can you credit it? Mark you the fond as in madcap fellow. Unbelievable. I really don't know why I'm telling you this. I've no idea why I'm making such an issue of it, why it gets under my skin so badly. I should have thrown him out straight away, told him "Clear off, you rotter" & all of that, lickety-split. What a remarkable personage. What an absolute bore he is, what a quiz! Astonishing, the things people will get up to, if you let them. One begins to think one knows nothing at all about human nature. Absolutely zilch. I mean...I'm not quite sure I do know what I mean...is what I mean. Oh, bollocks! You know, an odd thought occurred to me, husband—one to do with curious parallels. For we wage war no less valiantly—here in the no less important domestic realm, a different but no less substantial or germane theatre of operations & thwarted cooperations. For we women— the I daresay attractive ones, *id est*—must needs go fending off untold desperate foes of the frisky variety. Coming at us as they are wont to do sometimes, when we are all but defenseless against them whilst our brave spouses labor in no less dire fields of glory. Perhaps I overstretch my metaphor, but still. & as for obtuse & positively wicked & unconscionable Marius (he is most villainous, methinks, in something of a benign & charming way, I reckon—or perhaps not, perhaps it's just my imagination), the campaign, nay war, he makes 'gainst my treasured honor & chaste treasure (my cunt, is what I'm trying decorously to say here) is under weigh & no mistake. I do hope it's all in jest on his silly part; him having fun; a cod siege, as it were. He is an awfully nice chap, after all, so merry & sweet & nice & kind & musical & considerate & quite sunny & cheerful (at least he used to be) & not all that bad-looking for a shorty-short short guy with a hairline that reminds one of last year's economy (*id est*, it's greatly "in recession") if a bit dorkish & certainly goofy. When the servant brought him the cup of honey he wanted, it was filled up to the brim—perhaps one of cook's private jokes; & he (Marius) held it up &

smiled & said "A cause of you, dear Lora dear, & your p-p-pronounced pu-pu-pulchritude, one's c-c-cup surely ru-ru-runneth over!" Boy did that crack him up. Him a-slapping his knee & busting up like it was the most riotously uproarious & corkerish thing anybody in the history of comedy's ever said in the history of comedy & most downright hilarious & clever-dick godsdamned if it wasn't the funniest thing imaginable, like he was quoting what's-his-name, that playwright, that Greek, whose name escapes me right now & that'll probably come to me in the middle of the night like a ghost or one of the kiddies who can't sleep or like one of your wet dreams. You're not having wet dreams still are you, Caius Aquilla? I certainly hope not. He's just very lonely, surely, Marius. A bit smitten. & who am I to say thee (as in "him") nay? Of course he's a chauvinist through & through. Of course he's quite the insouciant valetudinarian. Doesn't have to work a stitch, really. Lawyer in name only now. Filthy rich & all of that. Hence the strange, blithe hobbyist proclivities & what not. His insipidities! How might one countenance them? Insupportable that he's so insensitive to them; & of course he's a superpig & megalech. All you Roman men are. Goat-randy to a man. I mean, come on. One wonders if the days when people had a modicum of manners are over. Such riff-raff everywhere. They're coming in the windows, scaling the walls. But he *is* our neighbor, after all. I will say that much for him. & lost his dear wife, as you know, only just this Januarius—poor fellow, poor fool, stupid eegit. I dunno what I would do if I lost you, wheat muffin. Surely I should want to die, hope to, too. I wouldn't be able to bear it, surely. How could I? I'd have to top meself, I would. I wouldn't be able to carry on. I wouldn't. Speaking of topping oneself or the prospect thereof, I can never decide if I'd rather take poison or have someone stab me through the breast, the heart, if I ever had to do the noble, honorable Roman thing &—you know—commit suicide. Such a conundrum, really. It is & no mistake. All the time I wonder: did Cleopatra really let an adder bite her or is that just some bloated, scurrilous urban myth? I'm serious. I'd like to know. Honestly, I would. It's like that jejune question we'd as kids ask ourselves about whether, had we the choice, we'd rather be deaf or blind. How very morbid I am sometimes. Like, the other evening? Well, Drusilla asked me if I shouldn't prefer, one day, to visit Londinium or Alexandria, & I said: "Heavens, what in the world for, Dru?" "Oh, you know, to travel," said she. "See the world a bit. Get a new perspective on things & that sort of thing!" As if that were a good thing! What a notion! Why would anyone save a lunatic want to leave Rome?! What sort of response can one give to such a sally? Leave Rome? Unthinkable! Unless, natch, it was/is to do what you do, valiant, peripatetic husband. Of course. I'm not saying anything bad about *that*. About our military & all of that, you know. Our serving men, our warriors. About campaigning & colonizing & cutting off barbarian heads & having their tongues out & crucifying them for fun & to make them bow down to Imperial Rome & so forth. No, sir—& we thank you & bow down to you & honor you for your service. Ah, Hades. I'd better have a nice hot bathe now, with heaps of bath salts & rosewater & lavender & civet, try & halt these terrifically as I said morbid caravans of thought & then go & see how our dear children are faring, the little darlings, little precious ones, wee overachievers. I don't mean to be (or come off as) so very ostentatiously doting & fawning but, gosh, if you saw the way they play with each other these days & heard their serious little sharpish-shrill voices raised when they're furious in earnest about something, their terrible-wonderful tempers flaring, you'd wax sentimental too, I think. So, *so* precious, both of them. They could not be cuter, either one of them. & me so proud of them, as I know you very are. Julia'd wandered into the kitchen the other day & I went to fetch her, right? Well, in the hot heat of the place, cook had, well, she must have begun to pong a bit, I think. & as I came running in, Julia, who was standing looking up at cook with her pits & her great fat brow all wet with sweat—Julia goes: "Mummy, Mummy!' & I said "What's the commotion, lamb? What's the matter here?" "Mummy, I smell gorgondzoldla [sic]," says she. I just about laughed my head off at that one! "Gorgondzoldla!" Hahaha! That kid, so funny. Cook could have died, I daresay, from mortification. Hard at work she was indeed—making a roux of some sort, I reckon. Stinky work. I'll warrant I just cackled like a mad thing & bid Jules come away with me, away from the smell of rank cheese that effused from her (cook's) person! Ahahaha! Oh the little darlings. They do make me laugh so that I'm fit to be tied, as the saying goes. They've had a rough week, though, you know, what with Fido dying & them seeing that slave badly as in indecently whipped, the poor sweet dears. Still & all, we're all of us in fine fettle & you needn't worry a jot. Or just a jot & that's all, no more. Take care, come back safe, safe as houses, write soon, keep your guard up, & your pecker up, & your head down when you're attacking, dear friend. Kiss-kiss & miss you very muchly, sure as I am

Your Lora Caecilia

P.S. Reading over your last I came across the bit where you wish me to recount our nuptials. Perhaps another time. I find I'm in a bit of a pet, kind of vexed & in a wax & haven't a mind to do it just-the-now. Forgive me, husband. I revile him, if you must know, & his astonishing advances. I bemoan my state, my maybe-fate, of perhaps succumbing to his most unwelcome & quite tempting overtures & strategems upon my person.

P.P.S. What d'ye think he meant by "redheads?" I don't mean to come off as peevish or petulant or anything, but still. Surely my hair is brown with tinges only of random auburn. I wonder if he's colorblind as well as... What *do* you call someone who stammers? A stammerer, I imagine. Almost onomatopoeic, I should say. Huh. But the question of whether he's a stammerer or a stutterer remains. I fear I may have given you too much of this quote-unquote good neighbor, but I find myself in a state of semi-fascination over him—his quirks & queer manner, at least.

P.P.P.S. Aeschylus! No—Aristophanes. That's right.

I MARS

Dear Friend:

Hail! How are you? Hope you are doing fine. Kids, too. How am I? I'm all right. Marcellus isn't, however; in fact, he's dead. I'm starting to think that being my tentmate's a bad fate and a very bad fate indeed. First Beefy, now him. They've given me a new guy, Domitus, whom I'll tell you about in a sec. Marcellus—he got it in the neck. Absolutely brutal. It wasn't even during a fray, but when we were traipsing home (how it burns to write that word—what I mean is, as we were clomping back to base camp). We alighted upon a lovely rushing stream, the water so clear and tempting-looking on a (they say unseasonably) hot and muggy, sweltering day. Spotting limpid water, Marcellus took off a-running, crow-hopping and skipping and flapping his arms like a giant bird, to make the other lads laugh, I imagine; flung his helmet away from him theatrically; and about five seconds after he bent then splayed himself out to drink/dunk his head in the frothing currant, an arrow zinged *zing!* right straight into his effing neck. Fast as you can say, "Look out, mate! There's an arrow headed toward your head!" out of bloody *nowhere*, the thing came. What a shot: spectacular. As we've seen heavy action three days in a row now (the enemy had catapults—gods know where the godsforsaken savages got them; it really slows things down in terms of us just mowing them over, when they have artillery of some sort like that), we didn't go a-chasing after the yodeling hordes who cried alas and fled like cowards, retreated or whatnot. Normally we rush after them, so as to cut them to bits and have some extra fun, but the generals, I reckon, reckoned that we'd had enough for one day and moreover that that might be a clever tactic, a trap, on the enemy's part: they run away, then lead us to some gully or gulch or valley where they're waiting to—here's a new word I learned—*ambush* us. I guess it means to come out of some bracken or from behind a boulder or deep, dark wood and attack, pop out from behind a hedge or a huckleberry bush or something, I don't know, and start smiting. Hide then strike. Ambush—what a funny old word. "We were ambushed." Pretty efficacious plan or ploy, if you ask me, if unconventional and not exactly *comme il faut*. So anyway, there's us, all happy we got to knock off for the day, dismissed and looking forward to having some "free time" for picking wildflowers (honeysuckle, bluebells, buttercups, hyacinth) or floundering round or splashing each other in the many opalescent ponds and streams and waterfall/pools and rivers they've got going round here—and that's when Marcellus got, well, knocked off. We'd stopped for a break, in a clearing, just before Mar saw the water through a clump of tall trees; I had closed my eyes for a mere second or two, taking in the glorious warmth of the sun, looking up at it, the sun, with eyes closed—it gives you a funny feeling, doesn't it? I opened them just in the nick, looked over, and saw the whole bleeding thing. I must've blinked around twenty times in a row: I couldn't believe what I was seeing. Thing was, on our way back an owl had just hooted in the middle of the afternoon. Three allegorical times, it did. Gave me the howling fantods like anything. We should have known something was amiss, something not-good was going to happen. Never a good omen, an owl calling in midday. About the worst thing that *could* happen. Save, of course, an arrow getting you—and right smack in the neck, no less—while you were simply taking a simple sip of river water. When the owl had *hoo-hoo'd* his *hoo-hoo* we all sort of stood there stock still for a second; only brave-foolish Marcellus laughed it off, curiously: "You guys are so bloody superstitious," he sniffed. "It's only a hoary old hoot owl. Bad luck? Wives tales for the credulous! An harbinger of absolutely nothing; a flat-faced bird that calls out to find mates—just like a meretrix might in old Rome or anywhere you find them. Why do you lot look so glum and stuff? Really! Come on now, lads, let's make haste and get back: I'm well hungry, quite famished—aren't you? When's the last time any of us had a meal or even a snack? Breakfast was yonks ago! Let's go. Come on. Let's hustle." I daresay he *would* bid us sally forth and *toute de suite*. "Up,

up, you lazy buggers," said he. "Make haste!" said he. Make haste to
hasten his own demise, is more like it, poor old soul. What if he had said
instead, "How 'bout we kick back for a spell by this placid, viridescent
meadow, find a stream to skim stones in, have a spot of lunch (well, a
snack, rather, as we grunts don't carry lunch with us on fray days, it not
being a great idea, the generals think, for us to even contemplate the idea
of quitting fighting in the middle of a battle in order to sit down and
refresh ourselves with a full meal) and a wee lie-down, just for a violet
hour or so, knit our war-roughened hands behind our valiant, sword-
heaving heads, forget the hot gates, the nicks and cuts of the day's fray, the
dust and the guts and the blood gushed and enjoy the dream music of this
sweet emerald burbling stream, huff deliciously the fulsome and refreshing
breath of these innumerable wildflowers, that night-blooming jasmine,
those beeches and birches, yellow willows, gorse, eucalyptus, amaryllis, ice
plant soughing in the slight warm wind?" Had he done so, suggested such
a thing, he might just be alive and kicking right now, raffishly telling us a
tall tale, laughing mirthlessly, or keenly gnawing a roasted turkey leg or
picking at his bum and making a scrunchy face of some sort, something
sure to put anyone off their food, even a base Iberian. The enemy archer
who got him might've headed back to *his* base camp, missed seeing us
completely, had a snack himself of some sort (barbarians surely must eat
something—I've never asked one what they munch on, seeing as we've had
a "No Quarter" order for months now and take no prisoners ever never),
and he, Marcellus, would be here right now, munching a sugared or salted
loaf or an handful of pig jerky, making a joke at someone's expense.
Mine, for instance. We're all of us completely nonplussed, I can tell you
that much. We're constantly aware of it, its possibility, nay, probability,
and never ready for it, really, the death of a comrade, how one day
someone's right here, the next he's being buried or burnt. Marcellus, gods
rest his bumptious soul, was a good mate, a good guy, a good soldier, a
good laugh, too. I must've gone spinach green, seeing him flopped forward
into the water, him with a feathered lance in his neck, the red blood like

wine turning the stream pink. Had to marshal my every nerve just to cope. Very sad to see him go. Very, very sad, am I. But now the lads, esp. this Domitus, look at me askance like I'm some curse somehow, worse than a chorale of owls first thing in the morning: "Good luck, Dom," one wag yodeled when Lieutenant Optio assigned him my way; "Nice knowing ya, mate!" the guy fluted, hooted, cackled afterward. Ouch. Ouchly. The guys can be so unfeeling sometimes. Moving his kit slowly over, Domitus, mincing in, all pallor and sweat, flashing a sweet shy smile said: "Lookee here, Caiuth Aquilla, if you don't mind too terribly horribly much I think I'll just move my cot outside and thtuff. I thure hope you won't be frightfully offended, old man. I mean, I thall keep my gear in here, all regulationlike and whatever, but I'll thleep outside, I think. No offenth and I hope you underthand, but... It's just...well...cheerth, anyway..." I felt so bad. So sad. So low. He couldn't even look me in the face, poor fellow. Like I was poison, he looks at me. Like I was about as much fun as cold soup or a full latrine; as licking a whole coat of bright yellow paint fresh off the wall of an underground privy in central Constantinople would be. Trepidatiously, and with the most distressingly deferential tone, he, Dom, pursed his mouth, said: "Maybe you could thacrifice a crow or a thnake or thomething like that." You can tell he's really quite scared to think that there's some demonstrable and irrefragable connection between rooming with me and being "next," as it were. Dreadful. Completely dreadful. I don't know what to say—to him or anyone. Anyway, just a short letter this time; I will write more soon. I'm just a bit down right now, love. Lovingly, dourly,

Your Caius Aquilla

P.S. I love you.

P.P.S. *So much.*

III MARS

Dear Friend:

Worst fears realized: I *am* a curse. Imperishably glum just the now, my gloom coming in washy waves washing over me. Feeling like someone trudging through miles of mud, his life a muddy farce, rain raining down on him, making him slog even more muddily, horribly. In pain. Much pain. Hurting, hating self. Thinking: must have been born under an evil star, me. Or at the very least an evil/wicked/very bad comet or meteor. This is the thing: last night gentle, lisping Domitus was partially eaten by a pack of wolves or bears or something. And now he's bloody dead. I feel so terrible about it, Lora. Wracked with remorse. He'd moved his cot quite far away from our tent, it seems—very near the tree line of the thick dark and eerie-scary super gloomy woods near where our base camp is. The first night his kip was plonked right outside the tent as planned, but apparently I snore like the dickens because that morning, rubbing deep sleep from red eyes, he lisped: "Blast, Caiuth, you're a great guy and a capital tholdier and everything, real thwell, & thertainly one of the most handthome fellowth in the Legion, but I darethay I'll tell you thomething for nothing: did nobody never tell you you're a wegular woof-waither?" "A what?' said I. "A woof-waither—*you* know," he said and pointed at the sky. "Oh, a *roof*-raiser," I said. "Got it. I snore, I take it." Continuing, he goes: "More than that, Caiuth: you weally weally weally weally do thnore like a wounded wildebeest in your thleep. You were unaware? Nobody'th ever mentioned it before? How curiouth!" "No," said I. "Oh my godth, I like didn't get half a wink last night, for Thomnus' thake! What do you thuggest we do about this thituation?" "Thomnus?" I says. "You know, the god of thleep," says he. "Oh—Somnus," I says. "Got it." Then I asked him if he really thought so. "Thought what?" Domitus said. "That I was...you know..." "Handthome? Thirtenly. But still, Caiuth—you weally ought to try and do thomething about the thnoring!" Sheepishly, then, I told him I was "thorry" (that part slipped out, and he gave me a look like "weally?" and, feeling doubly terrible, I had to apologize all over again; it's just that it's too easy for me to imitate or mimic people—I can't help it, I'm a natural, it seems. I really have a gift, I think; it's kind of amazing, this gift of mine). Well, then I intimated to him that my precious missus'd never mentioned it or anything, my snoring. It really came as something of a shock for me to find I'm a snorer. ("My *lovely* missus," I said.) Do I? Snore, that is? I wonder why you've never heard me? I mean our bedrooms are right next door to each other. Were you, have you been, that is, too sweet and polite to tell me, love? How kind you are. How nice of you to keep that sad gross fact from me all this time. Or maybe you're too passed-out pissed drunk each night to hear or care, or a heavy sleeper or something—dead to the world! Ha! Anyway, we found him, mauled as all get-out, in the morning—what was left of him. A truly gruesome sight. They (the wolves or bears) must've bitten his throat first so he couldn't cry out. Very canny, those things. Wily. Cunning. Or maybe he did cry out, but nobody heard him on account of we are all just so dead tired after a long, hard day of slaughtering "barbs" and we sleep the sleep of the just. Or sleep like you do, Lora. Hahaha. So sad. Such a tragedy. Though is it really? The violent, gruesome, unthinkably ignoble death of just one rather dull legionnaire with a quite severe and obnoxious speech impediment? I do wonder. That term gets flung round too lightly these days, don't you think? Our good old Roman papers and town criers cry "tragic!" at the news of just about any old slag getting crushed by way of something falling from a workers' scaffold, a house boy mistaking arsenic for salt or sugar, or the death of a kitten falling from wall or tree. So what are plagues and earthquakes, then? Bigger tragedies? It gives one pause. So sensational, these our modern times, it seems! Everything gets blown so far out of proportion. Anyway, Domitus—I just can't believe it. Though everybody else can, it seems; half the chaps who saw Dom's corpse just walked away, shaking their heads and muttering things, unkind things, most probably—critical-of-Caius-Aquilla things; and the other half looked at me like they full well expected something like this to happen, their harsh-looking lips curling and/or pursing in contempt or spite. Someone clucked. Another one tutted. Then I heard a snorty sound like a rutting pig, then an high hyena laugh, then another sort of prolonged snort—a horse one, I think—followed by a kind of raspberry sound like a great wet flatus. A zoo of sounds. The Circus Maximus come campaigning. What in the world? Not a Legion but a barmy barnyard, no less. Most unamusing. Plus mortifying. Plus I-don't-know-what. Awful, certainly. For yours truly. Gravely, Lt. Optio took me aside and asked me if I wouldn't mind too terribly if I bunked on my lonesome for a while. "You know," he said, "the men are kind of...you know..." "No, what, sir?" says I. "You know," he hemmed. "I mean...soldiers are superstitious to begin with, Legionnaire Caius Aquilla. And the more I can allay any in-the-ranks sorts of fears, the more...you know." "But I *don't* know, sir?" I said. "No?" he says. "No," I go. "Oh," says he. "Huh." I mean, did no one think to stand up for me and say: "Hey, let's not put II and II and come up with V here, all right? We're at war, after all, campaigning and everything, remember? Horrid things happen when there's battles and quicksand and arrows and hungry and vicious legionary-eating bears or wolves leaping from thickets in the black of night, all right? And damned lisping fools who prop their cots on the edge of a lair or cave or den." No, the answer is. No one said any such thing. Not a peep from any of these people. Not one valiant brother-soldier to come bravely forward and say "Hey, old Caius seems to be getting the raw end of the short stick" or something like that. I feel so down in the dumps or the mouth. Sure: Beefy was stinky, Marcellus kind of callous (plus a diabolical wise guy), this timorous Domitus something of a scaredy-cat fraidy-cat, milquetoast, milksop, pansy, wuss, gaylord, gay fag, faggot, flibbertigibbet, foofy poofter, dandy, nancy boy, shirtlifter, pantywaist, pole smoker, queerbait, "bear," "bottom," bum bandit, bum chum, rent boy, fruit loop, Peter Puffer, young queen, ass bandit, "dirt road" ranger, legionfairy, Greek freak, yellowbelly mamma's boy, drag king, and bloody flaming unbelievable homo and whatnot, but they didn't deserve such freakish fatal fates, no matter the circumstances, I don't think. Life isn't fair, Lora. Nor is war. Though all's fair in love and war, they say. Nobody sits with me at mess now. Absolutely no one. Zilcheroo for you know who. I get grunts instead of hails at brekky, I tell you. It's ridiculous. I'm amazed. Lonelier than ever am I, dear friend; so sad. Oh well, I suppose now that I'm something of an outcast and pariah, a real live *persona non grata*, I'll have more time to write to you. About what, though—I've no idea. Describing battles, blow by blow? The shining armor and buffed leather; orders shouted, the terrifying thud of an advance, weapons clanking, javelins whirring, pennants streaming in tremendous fiery sky; ribbons of honor depending from the bobbing banners and the splendid, shining Eagles; the crisp crunch of the march before combat contact; gaping wounds and bloodcurdling war cries; the unmistakable sound of a thousand arrows zinging through terrorized air; the snap and report of the catapults, the wrenching noise of the fell cranks; the thick thwack of bodies falling like so many trees after the desperate enemy comes at us pell mell, cut and thrust; the mad ululations of our reckless foes; the neighing of countless horses—more like screams, really (esp. to me who lives in mortal fear of the horrid creatures); blood gushing everywhere, spurting, fountaining from so many manmade holes like so many human Vesuviuses? The mortally wounded moaning, groaning, crying, blubbering, screaming, pleading for water, for their mothers, for a merciful coup de grace, etc. The not-so severely gored or nicked hobbling away, dragging themselves summarily away fra' the fray's vortex, sobbing in pain? Never really my thing and anyways the apothecaries and soothsayers and sages often counsel us not to recount our experiences (even in our heads) lest we become morbid and slack. It's very bad, they say, for soldiers to do too much thinking about what they've been through. Very bad for the psyche, the spirit, and for the appetite—which we must at all costs keep up. One gets admonished if, after warring, one sits on rock or stump with head in hand. Someone's likely to come round and say, "Buck up, there!" or, "Stop thinking and start drinking, brave soldier!" or, "Oi! You there! Stop that blubbering, you great babby and fool!" Just last year, this one guy, Octavian, was slumped on a log after a particularly bloody fray; weeping, he was—I imagine for having gotten so many kills because he was really good, you know? A right ace fellow, fightingwise, and ruthless as could be. Lt. Optio spotted him chuntering and went over and put his hand on his (Ocatavian's) shoulder and asked him what the matter was, then stepped back, whipped him with a little whip or a kind of a riding crop: caught him smack on the back. No, lachrymose behavior is not tolerated in the mighty Seventh in any way, shape, or form. So anyway, I won't be writing up battles here, I daresay. And furthermore, that sort of stuff, recalling and recording the action—that's a job best left to the lugubrious historians in their pristine white togas and white cloaks and gold hoods, those stern, unsmiling men who stand there watching like human hawks or falcons, who hang back from the action. Which of course is only meet and right that they do so, that they are wont to do; I mean, they're not getting their hands dirty; there's not a chance of *that*. All they do is take dictation and admonishments and quotations from the majestic purple-cloaked generals as they the lot of them watch the show(s) frowningly from the misty or sun-kissed heights and safety, which is customary and as it should be, by all the gods and goddesses, on account of our ruddy well-being's in the capable hands of their battle plans, so to speak. If anything goes awry in the midst of combat, it's up to them to make momentous decisions, on the spot, and set things to rights, retreat or flank or attack straight up— or else! So no: I won't be writing about battles. Oh, I know what I could write about and what you might find interesting! I could tell you a few of the funny names we have for the savage and godsforsaken enemy. Those might amuse you for a minute or two. Let's see: any Mesopotamians or Egyptians or other dirty-swarthy peoples like that we call "Hadjis" or "Messies;" Germans are "Germs" or "Germies;" Franckts (sp?) are (you guessed it) "Frankies"or "Froggies;" Spaniards are "Spaniards" or

"Spannies" or "Espaniards;" Jews are "Izzies" (for "Israelite"—get it?); Picts are "Pixies." Who else? Hmm. Saxons are "Saxos;" Greeks are "Geeks" or "Gay Homosexuals" or "Bumsquirters;" Black Africans are "Affies;" not-Black Africans are "Towelies;" Goths are simply "Gothies" or "The Gothies." I'm leaving some out, surely. Oh! Persians are "Pussies"—that's a good one, even though they're not pussies at all; I mean, those hairless pretty boys with their long hair and sleek olive backs and well-defined thighs and stuff—they know how to fight, all right! Pretty funny, though, huh—them names. Think I'll take a break and go to the bog for a bit. Be right back, okay, Lora? Okay. Here I am. Steady as lead. All right, what else can I tell you? As for the grim generals, I have great respect for them and their hallowed reputations, notwithstanding their generally diminutive statures. I do. You would not believe how short some of them are, Lora. In mufti, just standing about or something, you'd think they were jockeys at the Circus Maximus or whatnot, not commanding officers of the Royal Imperial! Funny! They say that good old Alexander the Great was only five feet tall in his stocking feet, so I suppose there is something of a precedent operant and all of that. Still. Pretty shrimpy, some of them. Ha! Five foot nothing! "Not so *great* there, Alex!" Haha! The higher higher-ups? I don't know about them, really. I sincerely wonder if anybody does. If even the generals do, you know. Who are they, anyway? What do they do with their time, their prodigiously mysterious lives? You never see them anywhere. Ghostlike, they are. Sooner encounter a god in the clouds in the sky: they really are very rather mythological, somehow. Anyway, I have more close-to-home and understandably pressing concerns that have to do with me and me alone. To wit: I sort of went round to everyone, circumambulating-like, inexhaustibly bemoaning my fate, how unfair it is that I've been tarred, as it were, with the brush of unluckiness and cursedness and what-you-will. But not a lot of sympathy have I gotten. Disinterested nods, sundry shrugs, a grunt of "whatever" here or there, several "eh's," various "uh's," etc. Plus a lot of looks like "what can you do?" and "forgetaboutit." Little comfort, no relief. Plus one or two sardonic if not malicious winks from the saturnine or clownish types, the kinds of guys who spare no one, have nary a nice thing to say, i.e. grumpy in the morning, surly during the day, downright churlish after evening mess. Quite a number of blokes like that about. Irascible, cantankerous, rancorous, curmudgeonly, negative, naysaying, miserable, discontent, mean-spirited. Oh well, not everybody can have as sunny and happy a disposition and demeanor as I have. My first name does mean "happy," after all. I think it apt. My last? Not sure if it's fitting, really. Aquilla means "eagle," as everybody knows. I wonder if eagles have wives? Ones they love above all others. In that respect, I reckon, dear friend, I *would* be eagle-like. But right now no happy eagle am I, poor me, poor C.A. I was thinking, you know, the other day about how I used to be so popular, a likely lad, the quintessential golden boy. Or if not golden perhaps silver. Bronze at least. Solid as pyrite. Looked up to by several, known by many, smiled at occasionally, nodded toward. Now, no. No medals or metal for me. Now, if boy of any sort, am boy-to-be-avoided, boy to be avoided like plague and made crude and awkward sport of at mess times. This change of boy very upsetting. Very distressing. Not a lot of fun. What to do? Must do something. Can't stand this— camaraderie gone. Don't like. All jests, were I even in mood to make them, fall flat, on deaf ears. "Friends, Romans, Countrymen—lend me your ears," the old adage goes, as everyone knows. But no lending of such will much come my way now, alas. No lending of any sort. Were I to need a razor to cut my throat with I doubt anyone around here would even give it me! They'd wonder what the repercussions might be, how they might be adversely affected. Yes, it's that bad. I am very much in ill odor here. Is that the term? Ill favor—that's it. Malodor. That, too, probably. Oh well. So much for reputation. As for my former stature as pretty high, well, *Sic transit Gloria*, as they say. Ain't *that* the truth. Easy come, easy go. Therefore, home-and-lovesick more than ever is

Your Caius Aquilla

P.S. Feeling a bit better. Tell a lie, I'm great, actually. Have a sort of imbecile smile, in fact, plastered on my face right now. Can't seem to be quit of it, get rid of it. Too happy. Well chuffed. Why? Well, this: had a pretty bally terrific and enormously satisfying repast of piping hot goat and onion stew with capers and peppers and new potatoes and turmeric and just a rumor of cinnamon tonight as the sun went down, the smoke from my goat-breath, as it were, coming in great, piping plumes, billowing forth from my eudaemonic gob. For afters, I had just-picked strawberries and cream. The cream foamed over my bowl, I tell you, Lora. Delectable. Despite it's being goat's cream, most like. I took my usual constitutional, just a wee walk round campgrounds, nothing major, skipped a bit to keep in shape, waved my arms around and around, ran in place, jumped a bit, shadow boxed with an imaginary Etruscan, whistled a tune I thought I might try and replicate on my lute later on, tripped on a axe or pick someone'd left just lying there, dead on the ground, said hello to some fellows who were walloping their lambent togas on some thick rocks in order to dry them, a few others who were slurping cider and laughing at something, a foursome arm-wrestling for money, presumably (since cards and dice are strictly forbidden), and two chaps roasting a fat rabbit on a crackling spit. Someone just the other day observed interestingly that the Germies consider the rabbit a very filthy animal and won't touch it—like Jews and their deal with pigs. While the Frankies have it that it's a great delicacy and dress it up with all manner of sauces and spices and things. *Cassarole du lapin*, they call it. And put it in a pan. Haha! Never had it, meself. Tastes like chicken, they say. Why not just go on and et chicken, then, is what I say to that. Hmm. Anyway, 'twas sundown, so the pink-and-gold-and-pale red sky gave way to melting-beautiful pink-and-blue, then went tar black. As I've told you, we're camped by a forest, of course, and the piles of leaves in the mornings, burnished yellow ones from immense magnolias and purple jacaranda petals blanketing the ground with color like fresh-poured paint, with glistening dewdrops stippling, silvering the long green grass, make for a pretty picture. Mists drift in, then lift, most midmornings—the sort of eerie, unsettling, wraith-like weather none of us like as it's perfect for a surprise attack, should the enemy be so bold and reckless and sneaky. Tonight I was on watch, a night of countless stars, fields of them, beautiful as blue snow, dotting the cold black air. I'm writing this to you, love, in the smack middle of the dead of drear night—quite romantic, no? Plus I'm up on account of I am replete with worry, angst, anxiety, and restive restlessness, plus major indigestion and heartburn—I'm not quite sure why. Incrementally they blinked on, an immensity of stars, as I lay on my back like a schoolboy ditching an Astronomy lecture. What is it about stargazing that makes us wonder about our respective existences, why we're here, where we're going, and where we've been. Little triumphs and major tribulations. What we've drunk and eaten, too. I reckon I mention food and beverage on account of I can't stop thinking about that stew. What a godsend, the cooks sending over a plate of the smoking savory, how buoyant to the spirit, how chummy a gesture, a really lovely one. And just delicious—loaded with salt bits, the goat tender as anything, as you, as my affection for you, Lora Caecillia. They, the cooks, had some fresh kid meat they'd had simmering for a couple of days' mess, apparently, for the generals' mouths only, but they served me some on the sly it seems, a delicious treat and most rare. Most savory. I think they feel a bit bad for me, sorry for me. I'm with them. I feel bad for me and sorry for me, too. I really do. If I weren't me, I'd have given me a plate of goat and a second helping, too. 'Tis hard, 'tis been hard, 'twill be hard for some time to come, I should wager. Pray for me, my love, dear dear friend, and sacrifice something dear and meaningful, perhaps, if you've half a chance. Try and see if anyone about can scare up a gila monster or something like that: just doing an obligatory chicken or pot-bellied pig's just not going to do the trick here, I fear. The jaded gods'll probably go (sarcastically): "So what—a rooster and a house cat? How imaginative!" I can just hear Jove in the sky saying: "Big deal. Set ablaze something different if you want my full and complete attention. Nobody puts any thought into their pyres these decadent days! Ridiculous!" Honestly now, chance'd be a fine thing for (feeling) old young Caius Aquilla. Chance'd be a fine thing indeed indeed indeed. Agrippa, a centurian, finding me lying down on the job on watch, catching me with my hands stitched behind my dreamy head and mouth agape, gave me a stern warning, then poked me, hard, in the tummy, with the butt end of his spear, then again in the groin, but only playfully. It really really smarted, the first thrust. The second not so very much. Nevertheless, I got off easy: he could have had me crucified, he could. But he said he wouldn't tattle if I promised it wouldn't happen again. "And what else?" I says and eyes him suspiciously. "Nowt," says he. Everybody wants something for something these dark cynical days, Lora. "You quite sure?" asks I. "I mean, there's just the two of us out here, under the sky so pretty and swarmed with stars, with nobody round for half a mile," I says and sort of licked my lips wet on account of my mouth right then was very dry; and I think I kind of put one or two fingers into me mouth, involuntarily-like. "No thanks," he says a bit nervous-like. "Right," says I. "Of course. No worries! Nice night, though, innit?" "Uh-huh," Agrippa said, though somewhat coldly. Hard to believe, really. His magnanimity, that is. Perhaps the beauty of the night sky mollified him, the fine canopy (cliché, I know, but that's perhaps the *mot juste* here) of big bright pink stars above that we both stood gazing up at maybe shifted his attitude somewhat to the more lenient-tolerant). I stood to attention, snapped to attention, I should say, you see, soon as he barked out "Caius Aquilla, you idiot! What are you doing lying down out here on watch, you stupid bloody fucking fool!" Boy could I ever have been in real trouble, taking a break like that and going stargazing, plus lying down on the job, literally and whatnot. The fine meal made me so sleepy, is/was all I can/could think of in way of an excuse. It was only later that night that it occurred to me that I might have mentioned my gammy knee or my chronic toothache; or I might have said I'd come over queer as a result of such a rich repast. But then I'd have to explain why I (no favorite of anyone's) had warranted such favor. Such a conundrum. Thank Jove I don't have to present one, an impromptu rationalization, before Lt. Optio, in front of whom I surely would have been hauled had Agrippa not felt particularly forgiving. The thing about that, about standing before the man, as they say, is that the man in this case (Lt. Optio) has a sort of unfortunate frog face, one that gets all the more frogged-out when he's miffed about something or someone. It's really quite distressing. It's hard enough to look at him when things are hunky-dory without wanting to blurt out a croak right to his froggy frog face or go "frog face!" right to it, his face, when he's right there in front of you. The impulses one suppresses in the Imperial, sometimes! Whew! The myriad ways in which one represses oneself. Lt. Optio's neck sort of bullfrogs out and his already rather bulbous & wide eyes go very Orientalish when he's cheesed off. You half expect him to go hopping round (hopping mad) like he's leaping from lily pad to lily pad, poor guy. Fortunately, he's pretty even-tempered, and a fairly nice guy, to boot. I reckon he sort of has to be: can't imagine he's too much of a hit back home in Rome with the lovely young ladies, despite the fact that he's quite popular with the chaps, the troops. He'll even come over and mess with us once in a while—not often, but occasionally—and bring us some extra bread and olive oil. He's quite nice that way. Quite pally and everything. Nevertheless, I'm surprised he doesn't get into a wax more often, the way things go inevitably balls-up during wartime and with all the arseness he has to endure and witness and correct and chastise. Notwithstanding his palpably anuran physiognomy and even-keeled demeanor, I'd better not let that happen again (sleeping/ sloughing off on duty)—or at get caught literally mooning about, napping like that! Trouble does seem to find me, my dear, whithersoever I roam; it really does seem to seek me out—and find me! It fair stalks me, trouble does, and a foul fiend it verily is! It's like a dread, fell, prodigious knock on the door: "'ello," it says, trouble does. "Caius Aquilla in? Been lookin' for 'im all day, I have." Bloody nonsense. Bloody nuisance. "'e's not 'ere, mate," is what I should answer, but never ever or hardly ever do. Why, when I know that that's trouble itself a-knocking, do I go ahead and answer? Riddle me that, won't you? Why don't I hide or yelp "Go away— there's no one here by that name!" Here's me instead, every bally time: "Ah, come on in, old sport: kick your dusty-dirty sandy sandals off and stay awhile, won't you now? Make yourself comfortable. Want a snack or somefink to drink? How've you been, anyway?" That's me all over. I, Cauis—non-village idiot. I can just hear you telling me: "Don't let yourself get so down on yourself, Caius, you unmitigated moron." I have that precise voice in my head. Thank you for that, Lora. I mean it. You've never beshrewed me, really. Well, not so very much, you haven't. And you're incredibly supportive and kind and sweet and nice and I don't know what I would do without you, you know. Top myself, probably. Yes, probably just that. Deliver my own coup de grace. Fall upon my sword like the noble Roman I am. Goodnight, Lora. Sweet dreams, dear friend.

X MARS

Dear Friend:

Hail and thank Jove and Hera—I am vindicated. *Vini, vidi, vinci*—or however it goes. Or maybe *vini, vidi, venia*. There: that's better. I came, I saw, I...pardon. It's not proper Latin but it'll do, alliteratively at least. It didn't take too long, a bit of time, I suppose, but I'm back in the pack, your very bouncing boy, in the pink and also in the good graces of almost every mother's son in the mighty Seventh. Here's how. But before I tell you all my news, let me ask you how you are? How are you? I love and miss you so unspeakably much. I'm sorry if I've been preoccupied with my own issues and stuff, but as you've no doubt twigged from my few last—if you've even received them, that is; it's positively maddening not knowing whether these poor epistles get through or not—things have been pretty iffy round here, in terms of me. Pretty darn touch-and-go. Here's what happened. Oh, I can't wait for you to hear this, Lora—it's smashing, it's cracking good news! So: after yesterday's fray, one of the generals (one Caius Maximus), trotting his scary black horse back after the day's early show, happened upon a grove or glade where there was a giant wasp's nest—a really quite formidable one, with hundreds of the nasty fuckers, pardon my etc.—and it seems that, in raising his right hand to hail some other soldiers or halt his own party or scratch the back of his neck, he knocked the humongous wasp's nest loose, and it bounced twice then burst open. Crazy! I *know!* Oh-oh! It must've been his right hand on account of you must always keep your left on the reigns, they say; the left's the hand you use to guide your "mount" or "ride;" as you know, being terrified of the brute quadrupeds, I've never ridden—maybe one day, who knows? Part of our/my cohort (my little wing of it, that is), coincidentally, was trundling tiredly back down a dusty path that crisscrossed with his leafy one, and we converged just then—right when he swatted the blasted, humming, nasty thing. As I was out front, running "point," as we say, walking along, on me lonesome, friendlessly ambling (as is my sad wont these me-*qua*-pariah days), I spotted him first, poor sod, his horse bucking furiously and winching out of mad control and him being stung like mad as well, his *eqqus* describing a frenzied, crazy-eight kind of tortuous circle, with the general thrashing round and waving and looking like he was dancing or slap-fighting with an aggressive ghost or something, batting the air in front of him like he was trying to best Aeolus himself. Then he goes a-slapping himself quite violently, left and right and up and down as the wasps did their angry, buzzing worst, biting (stinging, I mean) the poor fellow again and again and again and again. Pure Pandemonium, it was. A look, I shouldn't wonder, of sheer terror on his face. Very eerie the way they only seemed to concentrate on getting *him*, the general, him and him alone. Maybe once, one would think, they'd hone in on someone else in the immediate vicinity? Get their target in their collective monomaniac little insecty sights and put their hairy little backs into it. But no. None of that. Quite strange, the world of nature, innit? So much we don't know about…things. Creatures and creation. Different beings and their doings, motivations. Tell you what: there was a murder of crows nearby (again!) and *they* sure did wing the Hades away in a hurry. Like someone had blasted right next to them a bolus of fire from a pussiant black-and-yellow catapult: the sky went fairly thick/black with them, their furious flapping. Of course the general's lieutenants, his adjutants, aides-de-camp and other hangers-on in a sort of I suppose reflex way just took themselves off, bolted, fearful of being wasp-assailed themselves. And who could blame them? Brutish, horrid, swarming, darting things. The sound they made was like a concert of hundreds of Eastern instruments all playing the same "off" note. 'Twas truly instantaneously very spectacular in a sort of horrifying way. Well perhaps I exaggerate a touch but there were many many of them, the wasps, a flying sea. Or maybe they were hornets. I've never known what the difference is. They weren't bees—I will say that. I know what bees are. As you well know, I hate bees. Bees are the worst. Can't stand the blasted things. They don't like me, either. I know they don't. Had they little bee-voices, and could understand and speak Latin, I could ask them: "Bees, do you like Caius?" And they would in a rather arch manner go: "Caius who?" And of course I would say: "Caius Aquilla." And they'd go: "Ye gods, no. We can't stand that fuck!" I know that that's exactly what they'd say. They wouldn't even have to give it a moment's thought. Hmmm. Rotters every one of them. It gives you pause, doesn't it, though, does it not?—the fleeing of the general's staff, I mean. Think: that these supposedly fearless grim men of savage war and bloodlust could be so knee-knockingly lily-livered in the face of a mere swarm of possibly a thousand hundred angry, deadly, flying insects. Ah, but in a pack or squadron—the wasps or hornets, that is—one can imagine how painful their needles can/could be. I know this myself on account of I was stung many times, possibly fifty or so! Maybe twice that! Moreover, we know now that I am allergic to bees but not to wasps or hornets. What I did, without thinking, apparently, was this: seeing something was amiss with a riding-along someone in a purple cloak ("It's one of the generals, perhaps," I says to meself), I took off running like toward him; I threw down my arms and, um, waved my arms arms—as though that would disperse or vitiate the wasps. Silly notion, I know. "Allow me assist you [sic], Your Majesty," I bellowed. I was so nervous and excited that I forgot to put "to" in there. I might put it down to the fact that the general, up close like that, really does have the most remarkable and charming-colored eyes: a very dreamy-crazy shade of lavender, melting-like and quite pretty. Still, that little grammatical lapse will haunt me for the rest of my very, don't you know. Really quite noxiously irksome to me that I misspoke like that; normally I'm quite articulate, wouldn't you say? I think so. D'you think that what I shouted was too grandiloquent, too much like bowing-and-scraping in a linguistic sort of way? I mean, if it had been grammatically correct? I'm mortified, Lora. Really I am. It just kinda slipped out, that phrase, and could not be called back for love or money. Perhaps it was pompous, or at least too presumptuous, but let the candied tongue lick absurd pomp, is what I say! And in the hot heat of battle—even against little flying stinging buzzing hovering horrible terrifying nuisances—one often finds one fumbling for *le mot juste*. A man of action (great action?) I do consider myself indeed, but a man of fine words am I as well; and proud of it. Well, to cut a long story short, I grabbed the little general's horse's reigns and then, reaching up, pulled him (the general) summarily to the ground and lay on top of him, covering him completely (wasn't all that hard as he's really quite tiny; you'd be astonished at him, believe me) with my person and my own crimson cloak (yesterday was freezing bloody cold—the weather in this territory's incredibly capricious; the sky just doesn't seem to want to make up its mind somehow) till the wasps were all stung out, as it were. Stung out on me, as it happened. Caius Maximus, I discovered, after I got up from lying or laying on him to safety, turns out, was covered in a coat of thick black mud, the ground under the tree where the wasps domiciled being very damp and mucky-murky. Well, that did for his stings, apparently, as mud's good for staunching them (stings), they say. Sooth to say, your Caius Aquilla is something of an unintentional hero, true purple. Allow me, by your fair leave, to dilate a bit on my new-bestowed accolades. At mess—after the camp apothecaries stripped me and dipped me in a hot bath of cooked mud, honey (is that kind of ironic, or what?!—or it would be, were the stings bee stings), fresh horse droppings, and the blood of seven chickens—I was knighted. I'm joking, of course. Haha! Maybe you bought that one for a second, Lora. Gotcha, then! No, no, no, you aren't made a knight just for lying on top of someone, more's the pity, or you, my love, would have to call me Sir Caius every night! Hahaha! No, no, indeed: no one's touched with the sacred sword of royalty and made a "sir" just for saving someone's life. Not even if that someone is a) a general and 2) about to be stung or stinged to death. The key thing is, the lads certainly are a bit in awe of me now: no one smirks or snorts when I strut by. Dear-oh-dear, what a nice reversal on the part of Dame Fortune. What a lovely turnaround. It's like the fabled Wheel (of Fortune) has spun backward somehow, backed up and spun my way instead of its usual rolling straight toward me, then running-me-over. A reverse sort of Wheel is it now, I daresay, and that's fine and dandy. The lads: yesterday afraid of—today backslappingly feting me. Yesterday glowering—today glowing. Yesterday pariahed—today invited. Yesterday marooned—today no Caius is an island. Yesterday… Yesterday…well, you get the idea. Plus, I'm out of them—ideas, that is. Plus tired as all I-don't-know-what. Way fagged. Understandably so. It's been a very long day, love. Just like the rest of them: tiring. In case you're wondering, even though I wasn't knighted almost all the generals came over to our smoky encampment last night (well, two of them did, at least) and, as I knelt and bowed, Caius Maximus said in a nice loud voice (and in front of all or at least half the Legion, it seems): "Let Legionnaire [here he looks down at his notes, squints a bit, then stifles a sneeze] Caius Aquilla no more be thought a curse and a dunderhead and oaf and dope and a bad-luck-charm-on-two-legs to the Legion, a [and here he turns and sort of stage-whispers into the ear of one of his adjutants: 'What was that other term you used, Flavius?' he said.]... Oh, yes, pardon me, a poltroon and miscreant. But let him be henceforth considered a good egg henceforth [sic] and a soldier valiant and true [he seems addicted to the use of hendiadys, him] and boon to the Imperial Roman Army. Let him—this fellow here—be considered a legionary of slight distinction and initiative and, uh, quickthinkingness. For however utterlyfatuous and inexpert, bumbling and incompetent, foolhardy, prolix, uxorious, useless, rubbish-at-most-things, dull, thick, gormless, clueless, useless (I think I said that), utterly *sans* self-consciousness and awareness; however much a lackwit, chump, a barber's block, purveyor of platitudes, sententious, and rather a bit of a total pseudo-intellectual, one of the very worst and lowest and stupidest and irreversibly idiotic and most doltish in the very best Legion of all (The Seventh!), hath he not indeed and bravely—and may we all huzzah him for it!—saved my exalted arse and most necessary neck! From stinging! And stinging much much worse than a thousand Persian diseases of the most grossly venereal variety! [big laughs he got with that one] Let Caius Aurelius [he's not very good with names, apparently] be acknowledged or rather dubbed or deemed a fool and an idiot and an horrid, nettlesome if rather beguiling burden *no more* [a few grumbles, some reluctant "here-here's"], but rather an equal to all men of his lowly station and severely limited, minimal abilities. Let nor man nor boy shun nor slight him ceremoniously nevermore, nor in barrow nor on barricade or at base camp! Hark! As a reward and as an indubitable favor from myself and from the exalted and most high command, Caius Adonis [again!] is to have two pieces of barbarian gold, plundered in the last fray, several extra rations of good black bread, a fistful of olives, a bag of golden apples, fat drippings with liver sauce, treacle, a large lump of good goat meat, a nice bar of salt, and double wine tonight [see: we're running low on provisions—so this was a great honor and my reward-repast made some of the lads, you could tell, drool with envy]. Let him accept with head-bowed gratitude and sincere humility this wonderful bouquet of fresh-picked flowers—peonies, actually, and red poppies, hyacinths, one orchid, and some lovely sprigs of baby's breath and a couple of yellow roses and pink carnations for good measure—I plucked or harvested, pardee, myself in, er, gratitude for his unparalleled and unmitigated bravery!" [or something like that, he said—I may be embellishing somewhat, but you get the idea.] A momentous ceremony, this. All huzzah'd, some hurrah'd. "Huzzah!" the lads said. "Hurrah!" they (some) said. My love, the cheers were fairly deafening—at least three or five were, at least (ha!); I couldn't stop smiling; a makeshift chorale of camp boys held prayerlike hands forth and sang an aria (the sentimental old ditty "Glory Be to Glorious Rome"); two or three of the fellows slapped me roundly on the back. One congratulating maniac (smiling idiotically and raffishly) punched me very much too enthusiastically in the most tender part of my left arm. Really nailed me one. Another crazed well-wisher gleefully-impishly mussed my hair then grabbed it on the crown of my head (I need a haircut badly; must remember to hie me to one of the camp barbers and soonly) and took a thick chunk out of it (my hair, that is, my wig, not my head), a fistful. There's a lot of that sort of horseplay and carry-on going round these days. Some bad wag started a game called "Tonsured!" where you sneak up behind a helmetless someone and pull out a fistful or so from their hair and say "Tonsured!" in the loudest voice you can muster, then run away as the guy who's been "Tonsured!" tries to catch you and beat you to a pulp. It's a kind of craze. The only sorts who seem to be happy about such nonsense are the bald guys—they don't seem to be bothered. I'm rather bothered by it, though; I've been "Tonsured!" three times this past week, and twice in one day two days ago. I'm tired enough of being guyed, you know, without this sort of superfluous silliness. It put me in mind of another game I don't think I ever told you about, that was played two campaigns ago, after a wing of the chaps came back from Hinduland or whatever it's dubbed. There, amidst the strangest of peoples, who rode elephants and magic carpets and camels like anything, there, I say, they'd learned a word—"shazam!" It means something like our "voila!" But much more talismanic-magical. Like what a conjuror—a real one, unlike so many of your provincial quacks down the marketplace or the Forum way of a Sunday morning—might cry as he made dove appear or a man's nose fall off (I have heard of such things but never born witness to them). So some of the lads used this queer term to invent a game where you went up to some unsuspecting someone and said "shazam!" and cuffed or cupped or clapped or clamped them in the testicles as hard as you could. Very crude. "Been 'shazamed!' have you?" you might say to a chap who was writhing on the ground, moaning-groaning in abject agony. I never had the displeasure, I'll tell you that much, thank Venus. How "ow" would that be? Well, you'll never know, will you, Lora. A) not being a man; and B) not being in the Roman Imperial. 'Twas all the rage, really. For a while, at least. Blessed by the gods was I not to have ever... I shudder to think of it! Anyhow, how quickly, mark you, did the general's moithering speech (about yours verily) drift from rhapsody to rodomontade to rhapsody again. Dizzying. Quite. It all went by so fast, so puzzlingly. Like something in a dream or nightmare. Rude clod or great hero—which am I? I used to think I was somedeal perspicacious, somewhat knowing-of-self in Socractic or Aristotlean fashion but now I'm not so sure. Lt. Optio reported that the venerable general told him to go a bit easy on me for a day or two and a half; also, I'm to have tomorrow off, get a bit of R and R. Isn't that grand? Well, turns out it's not all that special, in light of the fact that tomorrow's not an attack day nor is it recon or whatnot and practically everyone gets it off—but it's the thought that counts, don't you think? *I* think so. I'm going to sleep in till dawn, or near dawn, at least; sleep the sleep of the just; I think I'll spend the rest of the time plus this evening reading

Cicero and Seneca or Herodotus, or perhaps a somewhat smudged book of straight up Oriental smut the lads are passing round. Then get in some lute practice and perhaps some poem writing. I've been taking copious notes, jotting down little lyrical phrases—but don't really have a proper subject yet. I'll do some letter-writing: to you, of course—my dear sweet darling lone correspondent, dozing luxuriously on my cot, etc. I suspect they make them, our camp beds, so uncomfortable so that we'll wake up ornery and in a foul mood and want to kill more barbarians. Perhaps I'll go throwing a bit of surreptitious dice with the fellows, hang out with the cooks, play a bit of bloody football (you know I'm not very keen on nor good at sport) with some pickled Visigoth heads (rolled up in sackcloth) we have for the express purpose, then maybe wander about, keep my distance from any centurians (they're much meaner than any lieutenant or general), go a-picking strawberries or raspberries or blueberries or whortleberries or boysenberries, something much more suited to my gentle and imperishably poetic-dreamy temperament. They grow in such profusion, berries, where we are now. There's a plethora of them; they're everywhere. Their plump ripe bulging fruitiness bursts forth fairly straight at us as we trudge by any hedge you care to dip into to have a slash or a wank or an unmentionable (i.e. bowel movement). Anyway, "Thank you, sir!" I intoned boldly, in response to the wee general's engrossing encomium and so forth, snapping to complete and total attention, very soldierly-looking, I was. Most smart. "You'd have done the same thing for me, sir!" I said. Oops. That one, sooth to say, didn't go over so well. Lt. Optio, standing next to me, sort of deliberately coughed and gave me a stern warning kind of look as if to say, "Obviously you have no idea how to behave around the magnanimous leadership, you monstrous fool. Let's all pretend that you did *not* just insinuate that the glorious general is in *any* fashion your equal, confrere, or counterpart, despite what he said about the men having henceforth to take you seriously, you unmitigated idiot." I admit I was a bit befuddled. To smooth things over with a clever quip, I was about to add (on account of the general, as I said, is a pretty little guy, something of a munchkin, short-arse, shortcake, midget, toy-boy, vertical failure, etc., in fact) "Well, you and a couple of other guys, sir!" but fortunately for me and my big mouth my tongue stuck in my throat thickly—nervous, surely—and I thought better of it, or at least my tongue did for me, so to speak, and all's well that end's well. There's a nice phrase! I think I'll jot that one down as well. All's well that ends well—has a nice ring to it, doesn't it!

Any

old

way,

things really are

looking

up

for

Your

Caius

Aquilla

P.S. How do you like my little poem *qua* endnote, Lora? Very silly, I know, but it's just me feeling my oats. Oats with maybe blueberries and fresh honey and opaque goats' milk. How little there is to be enjoy, how much there is to be endured, surely, in this sad vast vale of tears we call the world. I wonder if I am the only person in history who's ever thought that, or put that thought that way. Nevertheless, it seems to ever-contemplative me (at your service, *madames et monsieurs*) that we must catch-as-catch-can at whatever felicitations, jollities, citations (in the positive sense), and paens from august generals and other mortals that come our drab, unmerry ways. Ah, philosophy. For all its bedevilments and vicissitudes, its drudgery and boredom interlarded with intense violent sudden-swift excitements (battle, that is), the Roman Imperial does have its compensations, however minor, however rare. The comraderie sometimes, for instance. It's exquisite. The friendships that last a lifetime sometimes—or till death on the valorous battlefield. I must say I'm tickled pink and simply very happy right now—as happy as I could or can be without you by my side. I should sign off saying Your Caius Aquilla Who Couldn't Be More Pleased Right Now, Who Couldn't Be Happier. Your right chuffed, tip-top, hunky dory, happy-go-lucky, devil-may-care, truly insouciant, living the life of Riley (whoever *that* is—I must ask around to see if anyone knows him!), an' it please your Lordships, top o' the mornin', never better, best pleased, pleased as punch, punch drunk on good will, over the moon, basking in the glowing captations of nearly the entire bally garrison, super-duper, sitting in the catbird etc., sitting pretty, etc., Caius Aquilla. Well, not *sitting* exactly as I can't really sit down very well and probably won't be able to, the apothecaries and solicitous surgeons say, for the next couple of days, despite the fact that they managed fastidiously to extract most (not all) of the wasps' stingers. When I sleep—if I sleep—I've got to do it on my stomach like a woman! I can't sit down to save my life! I've been writing this entire missive in fact, the entirety of this melancholic correspondence, with my papyrus propped upon a portable plinth, and me standing, itching and beefing and sedulously scribbling, painstakingly. Wait! Don't wasps keep their stingers so as to sting again? Were those bees and hence my ineluctable death knoll? If I die tonight, and this is my last epistle, know, Lora, that I loved you more than honey. Farewell, my love, my dear Lora dear. But if I survive, if I should live, please charcoal the aforewritten lines out so as not to be preserved for posterity—except the bits about me loving you more than, etc.

P.P.S. Please write soon. Am in sore (pun—albeit a painful one!) need of cheering news/hearing from you. Love you.

P.P.P.S. Had a dream t'other night I forgot to tell you about. Was being chased (me) by a bear. Well, first a bear, then a camel, then a wolf, then a squirrel. A squirrel? Well, a rather giant one. Why doesn't it occur to one, one wonders sometimes, to stop in the middle of such dreams and turn to the chasing animal and ask, "Excuse, me? Mr. Bear, Wolf, Camel, or Giant Squirrel? Just why, may I ask, if I may be so bold, are you after me?" But one never does. One runs. And wakes up sweating. Or screaming, then sweating. Hmmm. They say in dreams are prophecies. Dear gods, let us hope not.

P.P.P.P.S. Oh! It just occurred to me that I might provide you with a bit of physiognomy, in terms of the chaps. A grand idea, wot; and good practice for me in terms of typecasting people for my putative stand-up act—if I ever have the gumption to do it, which as I've said I probably won't. It's only a sort of phantom thing, a pipe dream, a reverie, something wonderly pleasant to think on. Latterly, I realized I've been writing away here, merrily or unmerrily anecdoting-down-the-lane, and sort of neglecting to clue you in as to some of the characteristics of my personages, my "subjects" and interlocutors, brother soldiers, fellow fellows, etc. Let's see: you know how almost everyone on gods's green, flat earth resembles an animal of some type? Facially speaking? You yourself, as you know, look a bit like a bunny, a very pretty bunny, I should say—to me at least you do! Well, windy Beefy, for instance, was kind of a fish-faced fuck, with great goggly eyes and perpetually pursed fish-lips; laddish Marcellus had a rather ovine visage, sad eyes, a big, aquiline nose, but with a wine-colored mark on his neck in the shape of a sea-star; Joc (my pal, who is known to you, of course, but I'll go ahead anyway and describe him) is *such* the vulpine type—intense red eyes, giant teeth, leering-like, pointy wolf-face, widow's peak; fey Domitus had a sort of egghead, his countenance accordingly sorrowful, as though his features couldn't stop thinking about how they were affixed to (ensconced in?) an egg. Who else? I'm thinking, I'm thinking... Hmmm. Oh! Of course! The little general I saved (the other Caius—at least I think he's the only other one—you can't meet everybody in an entire Legion or even regiment, surely)—*he* evokes a preoccupied cormorant. Or perhaps a Cornish Game Hen. Very birdlylike, that's certain. Rather avian. Beaky, yet somehow simian as well; so then you'd maybe say he's an ape-bird or bird-ape. Orangey-carroty Brutus you can already picture as an animated fruitstuff. And of course there's good old Lt. Optio whom I'm pretty sure I've mentioned is quite the frog-faced fellow. It really doesn't help that his neck sort of bulges and throbs when he gets in a wax. But that doesn't happen too often, really. Weirdly, the only one who seems to get on his last nerve is, um, yours truly.

IV APRILLUS

Dear Friend:

Hail, Caius. I have something sorrow-making to tell you & it's not going to be easy to disburthen myself of this heavy load, open up, tell you straight up, straight out, lay it on the line, & get down to the nitty-gritty; so I'm just going to come right out & say it. I muck or fucked up. I really did. Oh this is bad. This is not good. This is a major *faux pas* & a half. I don't know where to begin. Certainly, I never ever thought the day would come—the saddest day, coming where & when I never thought it would come; the day in which I would have to deliver news to you that would perhaps be most unwelcome if not excruciating to you, but, well, how can I put this? & now it's here. There's no getting round it—it's happening. Obviously discombobulated, I've let my syntax wax jumbled as a retarded child's alphabet blocks, & my thoughts are scattered like the tempest-tossed ships in *The Odyssey*. I'm sure you can guess what I am about to confess: so here goes nothing. That unutterably smiling, smug, unctuous, & attractive bastard Marius was here last night, mooning round, making moony eyes and kissy-mouths at me & so forth, after the kids were well bathed then put down & a glory story read to them of an against-all-odds Roman triumph over some pesky Egyptians. He'd brought his harp over: he wanted some pointers *gratis* from yours truly. Or so he said. What a sham. The ruses people resort to sometimes! Well, one thing lead to another as they say & we smiled & laughed & played & had a spot of wine &... I feel such a *swine* telling you this, writing like this—perhaps it's better if I don't tell you, better left unsaid, but I've started this halting confession so I may as well follow through with it, & plus with the outrageous price of papyrus these days I don't want to waste an entire sheet of it, you know, papyrus prices being inextricably linked to the granary stock market, as any fool knows... Well, as I was saying we had some wine, & some more, then a bit more, then just one more tumbler, & some deal of fresh cheese, a bit of black pudding, plus a wedge each of sugar-dusted bread loaf dipped in extra virgin olive oil, plus some pig leftover from the second luncheon time, with a bit of choice cold cow, thin-sliced of course, from a couple of nights ago &—hmm—some dabs of pate of duck, a plate of sautéed sand dabs, quail sliders, roasted new potatoes, a rasher of liver, plump red and golden delicious apples, grapes both purple & white, a lovely burnt cherry tart, toasted honey-&-nut paste bars, some manna morsels in milk & a wedge each of yesterday's moist-baked cream tea cakes from when I had Drusilla & two other women friends whose names I can't recall now over for a bit of chess & a deliciously vicious spate of gossip-mongering, the usual hen-centric get-together kind of thing, chitchat about this & that, a scandal here, a divorce there, banishments, sentences of death, who got the worst of it this week gladiatorwise, etc., etc. After we (Marius & I) got back from visiting the vomitorium (me) & the bog (him) & were settling down to make some music, we had a bit more wine & a bit more cheese & whatnot, a drop of cider or two—& well, I don't know how to say this so I'll just say this... we canoodled. He kissed me. We kissed, okay? Just a friendly kiss. At first, that's what it was: a peck only. Then a not-so-friendly bunch of them if you know what I mean. Full tongue & all the rest of it. What was I thinking? We were sitting across from one another with our respective harps, working out something in the Mixolydian vein, this diatonic workout or raga? The one that goes *dum dum deedle dee, dum dum deedle dah. Plink, plink, plink, plink.* You'd recognize it. & after a particularly good go-through, one where we were really in sync & meshing, getting along like cakes & jam, he stops & gives me that unmistakable, meaningful look men give when they're about to *do* something, take you & ravish you or go in for a gently genteel kiss: that melty-soft look they get when they get all mushy, or if their eyes glaze with frank, thoroughgoing lust. Blushes he & quite lamely goes: "Oh, Lora!" "What?" I says, quite sharply, me knowing something was up. "Lora! You have something on your face... Here..."

& I guess I had a truant, dead eyelash on my cheek & he licked his index
& reached over and brushed it ever so delicately away with the one then
another of his treacherous fingers, tracing, at last, the lines of my quite
high cheekbones with the soft back of his hand. "Make a w-w-w-w-
wish," he says & blows the lash into the very air, as the tension, the
atmosphere inspissates. Then he grabbed me, pulled me to him. "What
are you driving at?" I says. "*My* w-w-wish," says he, "is that you... would
be my d-d-*dish!*" he says & laughs, smiles like he's said something uncannily
funny. "Ha, ha, ha," I says, all dry, "very funny, Marius. Nice one.
Hilarious." He tried again. To kiss me, that is. He seems keen to embarrass
himself howsoever he can; it's almost a goal with him, a guerdon. What a
fool. What a prat. It's amazing. He's amazing. Never met the like, I'm
telling you. At once terribly flattered here & disgusted beyond all
comprehension. Quite at a loss with respect to what to do. "You are ho-
ho-ho..." he said. "Hopelessly beautiful?" I sallied. "Ye-ye-yes," said he.
"*I* know *that*," said I. "Tell me something new," I said. "I la-la-love you,"
said he, the fool. He made a play for my supple waist. I wriggled and
skipped away, giggling. He followed, faintly. I feigned fainting. He caught
me. I scratched him. He gripped me. I parried his thrust, as it were. He
clutched at me. I slapped him. He bit me. I bit *him*. He clasped me to his
huffing chest. I got a good, solid handful of testes & clutched them. He
yelped then swooned with pain. I broke away. *He* broke away. Came back
& clouted me upside the head. He grabbed me. I clutched him. He kissed
me. I kissed him. Full tongue, full on. He nibbled then bit my neck—
quite hard. I his. He clamped his right hand right smack on the wettest
bit of my sex. I pulled his hair (well, what's left of it, the straggles in back,
pardee). He embraced me. Cupped my bum for all he was worth & buried
his mouth in my cleavage. It was like mad dancing, two people drunk on
one another. Plus drunk on plonk. Then we looked at each other with
that look that comes over you when—you know: the way people do when
they're about to... you know. Then the harps went down—I mean, just
right over. His did that is; I just kind of set mine aside, but it slipped &

toppled anyway. & he took me by the back of the neck with his small, strong hands & kissed me very sweet then very rough & then sort of pulled himself together & made his lips, his mouth quite soft & of course I slapped him hard, but not like "hard"—you know; I don't know how to explain it. & then I said all the obligatory feminine things one says that one doesn't really mean *really*, like, "You can't do that!" &, "I'm a happily married woman!" &, "What do you think you're doing, you unabashed cad & unmitigated bounder?" &, "Who do you think you are, coming on to me like this, in this horatory & most inappropriate & flattering way?" &, "Just you try that again!"—all that rot that's obviously just flummery & folderol. In earnest I did say this, admonishing him sternly, firmly: "Stop playing the rake, Marius. It doesn't suit you one iota." He laughed at that, all right. "Ha," laughed he. "Ha. Ha. Ha." Then he grabbed me, pulled me to him. I slapped him. Mortifying. Blood bloomed from the cut on his cheek I'd made. Tears welled in's eyes. In mine as well, I imagine. He bent over, huffing & puffing, like an anchorman at the end of a relay race or someone who's been punched in the gut with a battering ram or the fist of a small but powerful & crazy child. Rose he, came forth, collared me (just an expression, of course; women don't wear collars), bit my neck *again*. I his. He licked my face. I licked his. I hissed at him, he blew a kiss at me. I feigned scratching him, then boxed his ear. He bled. I laughed. I spat in his face. I took him by the throat. He jigged a bit & brushed my raking fingers away, like a circus tumbler rounding off a tricky flip with a flourish. Then pulled me to him encore: "I l-l-love you, L-L-L-Lora," he said. "Oh, do you, lecher?" I countered. "I l-l-love you & I'm going to r-r-rape you," he breathed. "I'm going to rape *you*!" I panted. "Oh, are you, sauce box?" he said. "Ha! Chance'd be a fine thing! How do you reckon that one out?" said he. He took me, held me gingerly, kissing me sweetly on my neck, my ear, my cheek, my chin. Worshipfully, I knelt before him, his willing slave & concubine. He knelt as well. He touched me "there." Pressed his lips to my willing breasts. Toothed them (not hard, a love bite only). I him (his cheek). Next thing you know we're snogging like anything, making out like naughty children playing nurse & surgeon. Then one thing lead to another, & another, & then he took me & I was slept with him. I suppose that's kind of a euphemism, if not a full-blown one—plus a wicked & unsightly & gross use of the passive voice. We—how to put this?—fucked, Caius. Scrogged like mad dogs or rutting goats rutting. Fornicated. Made what I like to call the beast with two backs. & not just the once. Oh, no. But repeatedly. Hungrily. Ravenously. Perhaps that's unveiling/detailing too much? I'm sorry. I'm so sorry, dear friend. He fucks like a stoat, though. Really it's true. I'll say that much for him: knows what he's about, friend Marius. Marriage, by hymen, is really hard, isn't it? Not super easy. There are so many rough spots, challenges, my dear. Obstacles (there's one called Marius, in fact) to faithfulness & happiness and continued ignorance-as-bliss & all that rubbish. I wonder now: should I call you dear? Ought I, after what you've just been apprised of? Is that not going only to add flagitious insult to undeniable injury? Gods know. I mayn't be so dear to you now, I realize— not just this minute, & vice versa. In the wake of the fact that this kind of changes the dynamic between us, doesn't it? I mean, how could it not? As I said, I don't know what to say here & I am very confused & upset right now (plus hungry) & don't know what to think except that part of me believes (& I could be wrong except I seldom am) that in part *you* are somewhat perhaps maybe to blame in me lapsing sexually? I don't mean to demonize you & be a real cliché about this stuff, going projecting, but let me ask you: why aren't you *here*, Caius? Were you here, with me, this never would have happened! Surely Marius would never have dared make such a flagrant pass; & surely I would never have countenanced it, acquiesced, and given him my naked body, my tingling & quivering & yearning lips, & then gone a-romping with him, deliciously. I do hate to expostulate with you, husband/bastard, but you are, as usual, as has happened so woefully often in our marriage, away campaigning for the glory of old Rome while I'm being...while you let someone, a next door neighbor no less, conquer me—conquer me & take me in a way that I've never been taken before & that's left me wondering if... I can't even write it! Were you not away & fighting all these hordes of admittedly superfluous barbarians (why can't we just leave them alone, I wonder sometimes—what good's killing them in order to civilize them, & isn't that just a shade ironic?), it would have been you & me practicing playing music together, not me & him, him who's now my lover I suppose you'd call him or maybe paramour's more like it. Yes, that's a much more apt if not romantic epithet, *n'est-ce pas*? I cannot help but think it would have been you & me making love in all those rooms (if you were up for it, *id est*, and not too tired from slaying half the known world; also as a way to ring the changes, in terms of let us say the banality of our matrimonial couplings!). I'm a mess. I never thought I would in a million years be the sort of woman who...you know—what I just told you. "O, O, O, O," I cry like a redundant personage in a minor drama. What do I *do* now, Caius Aquilla? I have no idea what to think or do! It's not like I'm *really* blaming you, but kind of? I can't take all the blame here. I mean, I could take it if I had to, but I don't want to. & besides, I sort of never had a chance. He had my shirt off before I could get a shirt on, as the saying goes. You know what I mean—women in shirts: a preposterous image! Caius! Woe is me or I. Oh, dear. Gods help me, I really am as forlorn & forsaken (I almost wrote "foreshaken") as a heroine in one of those terribly melodramatic melodramas your basic Greeks were so good at back in the days before we smashed them to bits & crippled their reach-me-down empire, taught them who's boss & the new kid in town. Caius! He started running his hands through my hair like he was washing it or something, plus conditioning—with almond milk & spun honey. Then he goes cupping my lifted-to-him face, & massaging my head like an expert Cretan or maybe Macedonian masseuse. *Then* (I really kind of hate you right now, love; I am so mad; hate him as well, if that's any consolation, & I know it isn't, couldn't possibly be) he began to whisper sweet nothings of just the sweetest nothingness & telling me how young & beautiful & nubile & desirable I was, how he liked my plump rump & fine proud breasts &

bigger women in general. I'm not that big, a size nine, godsdammit—how *dare* he typecast me like that! What woman on gods's green etc. wants such a thing as that?! Then he told me how he'd always thought I was so pretty & unique & bright & fun & sexy & fetching & voluptuous; how he'd always fancied me & not just because he fancies gingers ("But I'm not really a ginger," I keep telling him—but he's just not having it, you know?). Then, nimbly, he started in on my neck. You know how my neck's *so* my not-so-secret weakness. They should make a chastity belt or I guess you'd say choker for the neck, for young, gullible girls & for godsforsaken, fallen, faithless women such as I, they should. It was like being kissed by the sun, repeatedly. Like eating a dish of fresh snow sweetened with plopped drops of orange honey. Before I could stop him or even wonder if I wanted to—I'm pretty sure I was very *very* drunk by this point, really just wrecked & giddy-as-Hades, though I'd only had nine or so good full goblets all told; not even an entire jug—before I could stop him, stay his I daresay wonderful, wandering hands & go. "Wait, what are you doing?" (like what every girl says when she knows *exactly* what he's doing: what do you think he's doing, you bloody ninny; he's fucking seducing you, you silly, shamming cow), he had my fresh white low-cut & most flattering evening dress down off my golden shoulders & he was lovingly cupping & fondly fondling & quaintly grazing & smoothing & tinglingly brushing the backs then the fronts of his soft-soft fingers against them, my panting/heaving/swelling breasts, & palpating the separate sides of my buxom bosom & then suckling them, my firm, pert (as he says "proud") tits, so sweetly & tenderly, one then the other, then both as he bunched them together & was able to get at each nipple in one "go," so to speak. I wonder what that's called, that technique, by the way? Well, no matter. It was quite pleasing & I hope you learn to do it one day. & gods almighty if he didn't keep murmuring, as he was clawing at my clobber, to try to get my dress off, that he loved me madly, that he couldn't live without me, that he'd wanted me for ages (from ever since we met, two months ago, when he, a widower and jumped-up nobody, moved next door to us), &

like a true Roman would fall upon his sword right there (though he'd have to go back to his house to get it; he didn't come armed, if that's what you're thinking—just brought his harp over, as I told you) if he couldn't have me, if I wouldn't give myself to him instanter & gratify his hot lusts & most heartfelt desires & blah, blah, blah. Pawing at me thusly, he was; & I all confusion. Ardor & vulgarity personified was he, playing the romping, passionate swain come to the lascivious city; me the quintessential tempestuous, giddy maiden. Such picayune pageantry. Stuff & nonsense. "I love you, Lora," said he. "& have done e-ever since I m-m-met you. Oh, Lora, g-g-give m-m-me some task & I will p-p-perform it—j-j-just so it takes me not so very f-f-far from you. Let me br-br-bring you s-s-some candied violets or some such treat. Please, L-l-lora! H-h-have you n-n-n-n-n-never been so very s-s-smitten yourself? 'Tis terrible, truly. Will you, won't you take pity on one who su-su-suffers for your s-s-sake? I'm s-s-sorry to g-g-give you any p-p-pain, but I am in mortal p-p-pain here m-m-myself, you s-s-see. I your very sw-sw-swain. Oh, Lora! & I *must* have you wa-wa-once before I d-d-die or I will surely, uh, d-d-die. P-p-please, Lora. W-w-words (w-w-which are the bane of my ex-ex-ex...life, Lora): how they f-f-fail me now m-m-more than e-e-ever when the o-o-o-object of my af-af-af-affections is right here b-b-before me. I l-love you with all my d-d-desperate heart. S-s-say you w-w-will be m-m-mine just the wa-once, & I will leave you in p-p-peace & w-w-worship you till my very own d-d-dying day & may it come s-s-soon, by Cupid & all the gods of love." Oh, Caius—his murmuring was murmuring much like you murmur, Caius darling, when you're in a libidinous sex-frenzy & can't control yourself. His eyes watered like the mouths of an hundred camels crossing three thousand waterless deserts. Or something. He wrung his hands clichely, he wrung mine also. In short, he wrung my heart as well, poor Marius. I was reeling. Never did a sweeter, randier confusion traverse my every sense; & though I can't say for sure, our sex often remaining oblivious to what goes on with our most vexatious bodies, I must have been sopping-dripping wet down you-know-where. Super sticky. Well, I of course protested a little bit, & squirmed some, impudently objected & stiff-armed him a bit as if to say "not so fast, Orpheus" or "take it easy there, Mr. Pyramus." To my credit, I should add. Going, as I mentioned, "We can't be doing this, etc.," he came forth all bold just then & bid me rise. Took me in his manly, beekeeping arms & kissed my turned-away then turned-to-him head & his lappings & bussings & little teasing lickings & salivating slaverings on my by-now fully firm & dilated nipples got more ravening & ravenous, him full-on gobbling now, just kind of honking down on, working his way round the hollow of my so-plump, heaving cleavage. He had them, my nipples, pointing toward Caelus, the azure heavens, standing at attention, saying, "How d'ye do?" & all of that. Then he sort of turned me expertly, like we were dancing (why don't *we* ever dance, my dear non-terpsichorean husband?) & lowered me once again & expertly, dashingly onto the divan where I had been sitting. I now found I was really getting wetter by the instant. & I knew he really really wanted me. (Girls can tell, you know.) I mean, say what you will about him— short guy, dufusy, goofy, obsequious, absurd, losing his hair, nerdy hobby, stammering like a stock character in a bad comedy, halitosis galore, etc.— but he *really* knows what he's doing when it comes to in-the-sack technique. I mean, he's kind of a love-Druid or fuck-wizard. A real ace-and-a-half in the art of seduction. Kneeling now in front of me, prayerfully-like, worshipfully, as though I were the goddess he makes me out to be, he got my dress up, hoisting it, so that it only looked like my middle & my middle alone was covered. Then he parted my legs very slowly & gingerly & took me by the hips, like some sort of madly excited & favored Pomeranian anticipating a meaty treat. Ever so tenderly putting his moist mouth on me, he proceeded to lick my wet essence, not neglecting the clitoris, the pudendum, the lips of the labia, & the softest skin a woman proffers, i.e., the insides of her thighs. In other words, he knows well how intense cunnilingus is, & how a woman needs a bit of suspense, a bit of a break in the midst of it, & that licking & kissing the inner thigh is a terrific way of teasing her & making her want him (& to want him to make her climax, orgasm, etc.). All this, & performed so passionately-leisurely, really meaning it, each luxurious thrust-lick of his long tongue—till at last of course I couldn't stand it any longer (you know how sometimes when we are coupling & you are going down on me I just want you to come up, as it were—come up, come up, & mary-come-up—come up & stop trying to make me climax with your uxorious & rather amateurish-by-comparison-with-old-what's-his-name's tongue, just go & put your doting self inside me & have done with it). So, thus, & therefore, to cut a really kind of out-of-control, dirty, wonderful, rare, & long sexy sex story short, I let him have me right there, quietly, right there on that fateful divan in the central room, the one (the divan, *id est*) that wants reupholstering real bad (perhaps zebra this time—cheetah's soft & everything but I am so bleeding sick & tired of that tired motif, I can't tell you). My by-now doubtless goosefleshed & stippled back arched in unalloyed pleasure; I was just ecstatically mouth agape from riding waves upon waves of unalloyed, undulating pleasure, my emotions haring all over the shop, my arms thrown over the back of the divan like I was doing some sort of swim stroke while bathing in the bluest & clearest of crystalline, baby-blue & chrysanthemum-colored oceans, letting the soft waves roll over me, caress me, swish me round. Mmm. He had me there—oh woe is me, Caius—then in my bedroom, then in yours, then the hallway (standing up, astraddle), then the bath, then in the laundry room (on top of the tipped-over laundry tub), then back in my chambers, him sitting on the arm of an easy chair, me bobbing up & down on his quote-unquote knob, his scepter, then in the kitchen (the servants being asleep in their quarters, oblivious to this marathon of concupiscence, this juggernaut of coupling, incomparable rapture, joy of joys). He finished (I finished) as we tripped or skipped (laughing, jiggling) back again to the central room for a while (him standing, *me* hoisted by him, almost balletically, certainly athletically). He's incredibly strong & agile for someone who's a near-dwarf, in fact! One wondered which thing to marvel at most: his prowess or his power. Then faired we forth outside to catch our breaths—& quietly so as not to wake the slaves dreaming in the courtyard with all the animals giving us something of a wide berth. M gave me a look that seemed to signify he would have me again, that his julius was up & ready once more to make the beast with two et ceteras. I smiled. He smirked. Dove we then back inside, got down on the floor (I never knew till just the now how much I love floor-rutting!), then he took me from behind, pulling my hair the way I like & roughly, like I was some sort of horse a-breeding, some wild coital Pegasus girl, him eagerly taking my rhythm, giving me his best (when that *slap-slap-slap* sound starts & you know the bucking gent's about to throw back his head & start in on his love-cries & sex-grunts, then shudder & come like a deified Caesar—all this with the greatest, most full & giant gleaming golden moon blazing in the sky outside). I wish I could say that it wasn't good, that it didn't mean anything, that it was just something that happened, two amorous ships passing in the etc., & that, by Zeus, we might or may easily have just been shaking hands or playing at taws or dice or hopscotch or hide-&-seek or something. But that wouldn't be right. It wouldn't be precisely the truth. That would be a bloody lie, in fact. I mean, I felt like baying. At the moon. Like some sort of animal. It felt so good, so right, so real, unreal. & now I feel so bad, so wrong, so false, unreal. I can't pretend to deny it. That I liked it & a lot, I must say. Now remorse is my only friend, dear friend. Remorse & gobs of candied pineapple & bottomless goblets of wine, wine, wine. How could I have done that to you and so thoughtlessly, effortlessly, readily, willingly, keenly? Noble you who've except for that one time with the slave boy when you accepted his offer to fellate you... you who've been so faithful to me & true? Are you sure about that, by the bye? That it was only the one time & that you didn't...reciprocate? I don't know that I could ever forgive you for that, Caius, were you to tell me you sucked a male catamite of a Greek slave's "j" until it spurted. The thought of it turns my stomach, it does. Anyway...fuck, fuck, fuck, fuck, fuck, *fuck*. Fuckity fuck. Damn it all & fuck a duck. Fuck two or three of them. Sideways. What can you do? What can I say? Some kinda real sweet billet-doux *this* is, eh? Nice letter, really lovely. Well at least you know the truth, the worst—unless Marius has some sort of venereal infection & has given it to me as a little "present." Horrors & perish the thought. Let's keep our fingers crossed & a few animals in mind that we might easily spare for a Venereal sacrifice. I suppose I should just sign off & shut up now & take a long, long bathe. Why do I keep writing, I wonder? Is it mere obsessiveness, a kind of graphomania, or do I want something from you now, husband? What could I possibly want? Atonement? Possibly. Forgiveness? Absolution? A kind word or two when I know I don't deserve such. Not in a million moons. With much love & no little chagrin from

"Your"Lora Caecilia

who

remains

a perpetual

puzzle

unto

herself.

P.S. I put "your" in quotation marks for the obvious reason that I'm, in sending this, not going to make any assumptions. He (Marius, that is) wants me to leave you, by the way. Divorce you. I'm not sure I want to. At least we'd be neighbors. You could pop over & see the children any time you wanted to. Hmm. Something to ruminate over. But no. I don't think I'd like it much, living next door to you. I'd wonder how you were all the time, make excuses to saunter over & have a laugh with you, play some new tunes, talk about old times. I'm sure I won't divorce you. I'm not sure I could do it; I don't think our Roman laws allow it. I mean, you could divorce me, surely. But would you want to? Please say no, Caius. He (the fool) rashly sent over an uncommonly beautiful necklace of immaculate topaz & opal, of high-grade gold & silver, that I think, but can't be sure of course, belonged to his late wife. How tacky! What presumption! The nerve of him! It's irresistibly pretty, though. I will say that. & it looks smashing on me—there's no denying it. It's simply impossible, though, I can't accept it. Yet I don't want to give it back. I'll tell him I misplaced it! Hahaha. Misplaced it in my granoblastic box of baubles. I can hear your quavering little Caius voice asking me querulously if I'm planning on seeing him again. Which always means having sex with him again—I mean, let's not kid ourselves. When people say, "I'm seeing someone," what they really & always mean is *I'm seeing them naked & they get to see me naked, too.* How we fool ourselves & willingly. We seem to live for it, exist for it, seize every opportunity to do so! "Seeing someone!" Ha! When what we mean is: "I'm in full view of them as they present, as it were, their private parts & flap then flop them right at me or let them plop or plunge them unceremoniously into me"—whichever applies. Oh you know what I mean. I'm not trying to be vulgar or revolting. It's just the way of the world & all. Truth to tell, I'm not sure I *won't* "see" him again. I don't really like him, but I like him. Know what I mean? *I* don't. Know what I mean, that is. I'm merely asking for information. Let's put it this way: I like the *idea* of him—which amounts to the same thing, does it not? Doubtless I like the idea of cruelly leading him on, that's certain. Messing with his head. & with his heart. That's what he wants, too. What all men enjoy. Thrive on it, they do. No different from a pretty woman's greatest pleasure: nicking another girl's guy. Mark you, that's dead cert. He's here for my profane pleasure—now that I'm "a fallen woman." Isn't that a nice phrase, as well? I'm still standing, though. I'm standing as I write this, using your writing podium, as a matter of fact. I go into your chambers from time to time while you're gone and bury my face in the clothes you left behind. Did you know I do that? Now you do. Well, anyway, we have plans today, Marius & I, so I suspect I he'll call for me in about ten minutes. I wonder what time it is precisely? I have to get ready. Let me go look at the sundial. Be right back. Oh dear—tell a lie, he's going to be here in perhaps five or so. Oh my. I'm so sorry Caius but he's just got something; he's got some power over me, & I'm enchanted by him. Transfixed or, um, transfigured—whatever. When I think of you v. him, I mean...things don't look too good for you by comparison. Just saying. The truth's always best, I think. At least I think it is. I will say that the neo-vogue expression "just saying" is, verily, a passage of veritable unmusic to my ears. Someone chants that egregious phrase, someone means he's "just saying" something mean & unkind. "Your breath smells like a dead ox six days rotting—just sayin" = just saying something not nice, something small & mean. Isn't it funny that that is just what I did have to say to Marius on account of he doesn't seem to be too terribly keen on cleaning his teeth all that often. "You have two left feet dancing—just saying" = just saying something disparaging about, in other words, someone's less-than-impressive skills on the dance floor. What I'm, in fine, trying to say is: I hate that phrase. I'm convinced it smacks of hostility, covert or overt, & I really really really wish people would stop using it. You go down the Coliseum, or over Mars Field way—"just sayin'," you hear someone say. You go to some spooky old sacred temple or to the park: "just sayin', just sayin'," someone nah-nah-nah's. It's too too crass & snarky an expression & it drives me flipping mad. I won't have it. It's the hilt of vulgarity. It irks me no end. All right now, listen, maybe the so-called truth isn't best, & honesty's not the best policy, as every poxy pleb & sententious, moralizing modern master of ethics seems to think. Gosh, I dunno. What do I know—epistemologically, that is. I'm going next door to check out his honeybee set-up, then we're to trudge up the Palatine hill for a wee picnic lunch. Ugh. Perhaps I shouldn't send this. Perhaps I should rip it to shreds, tear it to pieces. I'll give it a think. It seems rather unfair, me writing you like this; & as I read over what I wrote (& yes if you're wondering, I had to touch myself as I read it), gosh, I guess I could have tempered it a bit, but honestly, just thinking about him—I don't know what it is about the guy—gets me so hot, you know? & bothered. He's sent a message, over the wall, a note wrapped in a tube made of dried crocodile skin, saying he simply has to see me, can't stand this, can't stop thinking about me & blah, blah, blah. I'm a mess, of course. Flustered as a school girl. Giddy as all get-out. It's maddening. Please don't think me an horrible *meretrix*, terribly nefarious or something. I'm hardly that. We're none of us perfect, you know. We all have our peccadilloes & foibles & little quirks & quandaries. We're all fallible & we all make mistakes. It's just, some (mistakes, that is) are bigger than others. Big, big mistakes. If this *was* a mistake. Nothing is what it seems at the time, I think. Who knows? Maybe it's more of an omen than a mistake. A mistake-omen. I mean, the jury's out right now & stuff. & oh there he is—the servant's just announced him. My big mistake personified. I'd better run. Talk soon.

P.P.S. I'll write more tomorrow if I have time. Oddly, you are, at this moment, more precious to me than ever. I suppose that sounds rather hackneyed. Oh well. So be it. So it goes. Isn't that strange? Isn't life strange? It really is. So weird. Someone said—can't recall who or is it whom—that betrayal is the only theme. I think that's so true, don't you?

P.P.P.S. Don't think I will send this letter, after all. A bit hysterical, perhaps? Possibly. A girl "beside herself" with idiotic joy. Well, you'll probably never see it. I'm saving it, though. Maybe one day I'll send it, maybe not. Probably not. It's only much of a muchness, you know. I'm not exactly sure what that phrase means—I just like saying it!

X APRILLUS

Dear Friend:

Hail! A sad, sorry hail from your wife today, dear friend, as a sad sorry &
unfortunate (& mortifying) thing has happened: gentle, foppish, stupid,
smitten, fawning, rumbustious, offending, dumb-dumb neighbor Marius
is dead. Here's how: drunk as a March skunk, drunk off his ass (as in
literally, don't you know, he rode all catawampus & harum-scarum into
our courtyard on a donkey & fell right off of it like someone in a comic
warm-up act at the Circus Maximus), he, after he "dismounted," comes
fairly blithering into our courtyard yesterday—the bloody servants let
him in without my say-so. Clamoring at me, all of them every bit of
confusion and yowling alarm, they said he was fairly punching the gates
to get their attention, the cheek of him, & make them (the servants)
admit him. Comes he forth, reported they, then goes a-brandishing a
ridiculous little sword without a scabbard. It looks a right toy; & as you
know wielding weapons in the city—even in private, even after having lost
one's balance waving it while riding an ass—is utterly illegal plus it's super
vulgar if not obscene to see one unsheathed, a rude bare blade like that.
The servants themselves were crying, "Fie! Fie, Master Marius!" at him.
"Who b-b-bids me cease?! Who impe-pe-peds me? Bring f-f-forth the
m-m-m-mistress or ma-ma-master of the house," supercilious he intones
pompously, they said. Imitating him (cruelly), one comes running &
a-laughing, to fetch me; bows clownishly, to give more relish to his jest:
"B-bring f-forth y-y-your ex-ex-exceedingly pretty s-s-self, p-p-please,
Domina," one of them says, fleering like mad, hilariously. "A drunken,
b-b-b-beekeeping, dwarf of a neigh-neigh-neigh-neighbor w-would have
a w-word with you, Domina." Priceless. I wonder if they, some of the
servants, that is, have picked up something of a wicked sense of humor
from eavesdropping on me (or you, possibly) all day. But Marius entering
thus like this & causing such a prodigious rumpus & scene as though he
were a tawdry, overacting player at a fringe theater or (even worse) a cheap,
street-performing buffoon & butt's no joking matter. What the demons
does he think we are—ringmasters? The local impressarios or something?!
Absurd! That & our house a carnival fit to be canopied with a red & white

striped tent, queasy circus music issuing forth to beat the band? I didn't
know whether to laugh or shriek. The very thought of it, of him! Ye gods,
what can the fool of a man be thinking, if thinking he is at all? (He can't
be.) "What do you mean, coming blundering in here, you tintinabulating
imbecile? You're wrecked on wine, as well! Quit this courtyard pronto,
mister!" I say as I step into the courtyard, for quick as a cat's lick he,
Marius, comes forward frowardly, scattering the ducks, chimp, monkeys,
zebra, cats, chickens, yammering dogs, the baby croc (not such a baby
now) & parrots; kicking up plumes of sandy dust; reeling around like
there was a fountain or something out there to reel around. (Oh, there's
an idea, Caius—we should have a nice lovely fountain! Wouldn't you like
to listen to it burbling, like a lullaby at night?) I stare & hail him with:
"Marius! You muddle-headed voluptuary, you oaf & dope, you libidinous,
drunken n'er-do-well, what are you on about—swaggering in here like
this, & before noon as well?" Then, "Something-something-something-
something, Lora," says he & falls on his sword. Just like that. Nobody
could understand a word of his preposterous inebriate babbling. Blood
everywhere, just everywhere, all over the shop. Luckily, Aurelian was on a
school field trip & Julia napping like the dead (she was up all night last
night with a little sniffle, the poor dear: it's only meet & right that both
kids get sick like sickly little aristos, only peasants never fall ill, don't you
know; I'm glad they're prone to illness, the poor loves—proves they're of
good blood). Gods all mighty, what a mess & a half. "You bloody fool,"
says I. He stammered something as a bathetic sort of utterance, but I
couldn't understand any of it, sort of as a "dying fall," if you'll permit the
pun. "I'm sorry?" I said, meaning, of course, "Excuse me, you twit—can
you say that again?" But he seems to take it like I'm saying I'm sorry for
something I've done. Then looks he up at me with those impossibly kind/
sad eyes of his. Whatever could he mean? What could I have done, I ask
you, to deserve this? What hurt or harm? What a ninny, anyway! I wonder
whatever he could have meant by that, Caius. People—is there anything
weirder than them, dear friend? I am so glad we have each other. & I

appreciate you so much; I hope you know that, cherish it. I really do hope we'll never divorce—as so many young couples seem to do these dark days. You'd never in a million moons do such a thing, I know, as embarrass me with inchoate, drunken babbling, then quasi-public suicide. Dreadful manners, his. Bless you, husband. How are things on the campaign trail, as it were? Making lots of *converts*, campaigning? Hahaha! So funny. I do make me laugh, do not I? Well, you aren't here to do the job! Gently chiding, Caius Aquilla—just a way to tell you I yearn for you & your wack-o sense of humor, you zany. Plus I'm very shaken—& thirsty. Need wine badly. Gobs of. I'm trying to cut down on my drinking but this is an emergency. Obviously, there's been some traumatizing drama here, but it's all over now. One good thing: there won't be anyone to keep those bees of friend Marius's on account of there's no more Marius, so you needn't worry about them & being allergic & all of that rot—they'll die. Or migrate or something. I wonder what he was thinking, taking up beekeeping in's old age like that? Such a silly hobby for a Roman man, & him in his late twenties or whatever—practically a cadaver. Perhaps he had gone or was going mad/insane? Doing a full "Caligula." A lot of that going round these days, it seems. A regular spate of it. E.g. Drusilla reported that, just t'other day, one of their closest, oldest, most trusted neighbors was apprehended down by the Forum in a tatterdemalion tunic tarred with chicken feathers, clucking out a prophesy that, "The fall of Rome was nigh, we were a doomed civilization, excess & indulgence & convenience & abundant fruit & wine & imperialist conquests would be the death of us all, & that he was the quote-unquote Chicken of the Apocalypse, Doom Chicken, Bird of Doom, etc." The Clucking Cassandra, he called himself, I believe. Appalling. Just appalling. Just yesterday, Drusilla reported, the man & his wife had been to tea at theirs & had seemed fine—not one allusion to foul fowl in specific or the barnyard in general did he make. All this came straight out the blue—totally unexpected. Dru said he talked mainly of favorite gladiators, what he had to eat that day, what kinds of cakes he favored, how he admired her new

lace shoes & outfit & whatnot. The Senate Guard, she says, caught up
with him at home; he'd left a trail of feathers, so finding him wasn't hard.
Apprehending him wasn't diffy either, as he couldn't fly away or anything.
In the end, they took him away & cut off his right hand & extracted his
tongue. Served him right, of course, & most just, the very thought of it:
a madman like that going round freaking everyone out like that. He got
off light if you ask me. Rumors swirl so anyhow these days that you just
can't have people going around prognosticating gloom & assorted doom.
Not in a chicken suit, you can't. Guy had stretched a giant orange custom-
fashioned glove across his head, they said, to make his costume all the
more chickenish. People are on edge here, my dear; the public's mood
shifts like a sun dial. Mercurial as Mercury himself. Omens are daily
promulgated. Signs are divined in the very air. Most are hoaxes, I shouldn't
wonder, but still. One must think of the credulous populace, I imagine.
I'm no political animal; no avid follower of Democritus nor a staunch
supporter of The Republic neither, per se, but even I can tell that we
Romans are not exactly a universal favorite, in terms of popularity, other
countries-wise, principalities-wise, tribes-wise & what-you-will. I mean,
think about it: we *do* go round with a bit of an attitude, to say the least.
Sooner or later, some superlatively rebarbative quote-unquote people are
going to try & take us down—if we don't do the job ourselves, *id est*. It's
only inevitable. Alexander went down. The ancient Persians. Sparta?
Mighty no more. Hindustan, they say, has seen worlds of peoples be
buried under miles of rubble: an entire Atlantis or Underworld of Hindi
towns & cities lying atop one another. But promulgating such a thing as
our demise, the demise of *us*? Us! In a public forum, no less! & by a mad,
prophetic, *soi-disant* Doom Chicken?! Posing as soothsayer & clairvoyant?
La, what next? Drusilla said—can you believe this?—that the guy got five
fucking followers fucking following him home & vying to wash his feet
for him, salaaming at him & garlanding him with heaps of flowers &
garnishing him with chunks of crushed garlic & sea salt, then proclaiming
him "Messiah"—whatever that means. A low Hebrew term, I think.

Demarcating king, someone said. Cults of all sorts seem to start up right before your very eyes nowadays! You walk along, taking in the sights & sounds & there's some lunatic baying at you, talking nothing but cack, rousing the rabble around you that you're trying to skip away from, entreating you to harken to some nonsense or other. Before you know it—*poof!*—cult! I'll tell you one more thing for nothing, chum: it's never a *woman* looking to start a movement, though, is it now? No, sir. You ever notice that? We women, I say, don't go round (unless we are completely insane, & fit to be tied & banished) ranting & raving & caterwauling & lecturing & intoning & invoking & suchlike carry-on, dressed in black-from-dirt rags & with twigs & dust in matted hair, adjuring people to follow us to some island or retreat or ashram & begging us to just *give* them alms & bread. Men are so strange. Ye gods! For the life of me, I'll never figure you lot out. Take Marius. The only thing I can think of (in terms of why he—Marius, that is—might have been cross with me) is I criticized his technique when we were going over some Diatonic thing or other, practicing together the other day. You male musicians! So tetchy sometimes. Hahaha! Oh, well: I suppose I will have to wait till you come home to play duets. Or maybe I'll just leave off making music altogether, or for a while. I can't look at my harp now without thinking of blood. He was so nice (sometimes he was), Marius. Some people just shouldn't drink. & esp. in the mornings. Most people, that is. Which reminds me. Ha! Thirsty! Anyway, please come home soon, do, to your

Lora Caecilia

P.S. I got nothing, really. Just a habit, I suppose, writing these obligatory post scriptum. Hail & fare (& fight) well.

XI APRILLUS

Dear Friend:

Hail. Crunch/crisis time/mode continues: no less than two of our most faithful servants have run away in the dead of the heat of the night, absconded in the wake of the Marius debacle! Oh how I wish you were here to deal with this dire & desperate situation. All's in an uproar & I can feel one of my psychosomatic migraines coming on, the kind no potion or lotion or sacrificial slitting of throat of cow or goat will call to account. I'm coping, though. Doing my best to slay thoughts of unrest, to stay on top of all things domestic on the domestic front. (How my prose style wanders far afield. I must get a grip, keep calm, be strong, hang on—in-between crying jags & ragey flame-outs.) I asked Drusilla, via messenger, of course, for some leads on finding good help, which as you know, the economy being what it is these days (very strong), is so hard to come by. It's not always the case that such members of the *beau monde*, the *bon ton*, as she will be in the know when it comes to picking acceptable domestics, or at least ones who aren't too very sordid & corrupt, so I told myself not to expect much. All servants & slaves eventually betray one, as everyone knows. Recklessly, they do. Steal food, have affairs, commit murders, larceny, etc. This is a known known. So Dru sent over these two kids for me to interview. Blinking, abashed (as they should be), a bit hangdog like I'd already busted them for something. So very young & tender, too: they couldn't have been more than XV or XVI or XVII—& had that unmistakable look about them, fairly clean-favored & not unkempt, but like they were fresh-off-the-raft, as it were. Well, barque, I suppose. Barque or raft, then. Hmm. Not quite raft people—a cut above that, perhaps. Hence barque. But real live refugees of *some* type or stripe, nevertheless. A waif & an ape. Girl waif, boy other. A brother & sister— or so they say. They don't look too much alike. Could be from different fathers or different mothers. Hmm. Or perhaps in other cultures…oh, polygamy *is* the norm in some of them, is it not? Thought so. I had to run them through the slight gauntlet advised in Livy's *The Great Book of Hiring & Suppressing Servants So That They Work Hard, Steal Not, & Remain in Fear of Their Masters*. I shall relate here a bit of my interview, conducted with me reclining on my fainting couch, the plush red velvet. The royal blue's gotten so soft with all that lassitude I indulge in, admittedly, you're right: I really need to hit the gymnasium one of these fine days. Me couched, as I say, them standing before me, quivering sometimes (I liked that muchly), quaking, even. Question I [to the boy]: "You there, you jejune & bloody young handsome fool—can you read & write?" I asked the mouth-breathing cretin of a dim-ass dumbass, the golden curly haired lad, me a-pantomiming reading, then writing, folding my hands like a book, then darning the air with right thumb and index digit. I have always thought, I may as well add, that curly hair was a sign of lesser intelligence; I'm sure Drusilla, for instance, straightens hers—or has her maid straighten it for her with hot tongs, kitchen steam, orange honey, & diluted tree sap; she can't fool me. Shakes he his head, his lucent locks that fairly spray sunshine when they jounce & flip round. "No? You can't? Not a stich?" "No. Alas, Domina," he says, the fool, the stupid mouth-breathing bumpkin. "*Good,*" says I. "Very good." Literacy, I think, & I am sure you will corroborate this, only gives them ideas that are far too grand for their pleby heads. Besides, with all our precious books lying round, what a temptation for them, to pick them up & thus put down their tasks. Not having that one bit. Imagine a slave or servant touching one of your texts, Caius? Horrors, of course. As bad as catching one putting his or her pert/impertinent bottom on one's bed! "Question II: What about you, slut? Are you lettered?" I says as I turns to the bashful girl, trying not to oogle her nubile bosoms, trying not to think about her lips, their gorgeous symmetry, their plump, ripe, full, lush, bee-stung, feather-lined perfection. "I know my numbers, Domina," says she ever so gently, ever so softly, & looks down, all coy & replete with eyelash-batting punctilio. Goats &

monkeys! Flabbergasted, I was. The odd thing is, save when she's a-fluttering them, her eyes, she looks like her great staring orbs never do close; & with her turned-down, provocatively contemptuous mouth & sweet cheekbones tall as Etna, she, as I'm a person, looks a right little lady, a gentlewoman & not the obvious peasant she indubitably is. Perhaps they're both descended from unacknowledged noble lines. They're certainly pretty enough to be well-born; it is very strange. How well & truly-sincerely I wish & wish you were here to see them, observe their ways. "Excellent," I tells her & stands up & takes her sharp by the fine chin, a-stroking it. I could feel the fool boy fidget slightly, the sly, burr-haired, smiling-stupid hirsute eegit. He's no brother o' hers. They aren't related any more than you or I. He's rogering her nightly or my initials aren't L.C. She looks me right in the face! What infernal effrontery! How brazen! I smile, & cock my head at her, all the more in overt, cruel appreciation of her loveliness, the stupid-beautiful lithe little nymph. "Let's have a wee look at you, girl," I says, you know, by way of sizing her up. Flinches she not. Then, turning to the boy & holding my gaze there, I ask (in I must say a quite commanding & queenly voice): "Question II [to both, me looking back & forth between them]: Thieves, are you? Going to steal from my larder, my household, snaffle food from out the innocent mouths of my two noble-born & precious, brilliant children?" "Oh, no, Domina," says they, in tandem like, a sort of a vaudeville act/kind of motif: I half-expected them to perform a dance routine right there. "The alacrity & unthinkingness with which you have answered bespeaks your probably—I mean probable—proclivity for purloining," says I tartly. "Huh?" the one, the idiot boy, so insolent, says flatly. "How dare you speak to me in that rude tone, presumptuous & brazen urchin!" says I, & rightly. "I meant, like, 'What, Domina?'" goes cheeky he. *The very nerve of the youth of today!* I thought to my livid self. Then did I issue this unequivocal check: "You cursed rapscallion, you abominable right bastard son of a low-born slave of a spent Basque whore," says I. Third & Final Question— going strictly by the book, as one doubtless should—being as follows:

"Use a sentence in which you accuse & abuse the potential new hire, making sure to insert a possible nationality or race so that said putative servant will possibly proudly correct you & clumsily reveal the origin of his/her inferior nativity." "Forgive me, Domina. Yes, Domina," he says & bows low as he can go—quite prettily, actually, damn his epicene facial expressions, his soft speech, his darkly sparkling dreamy-pretty eyes. "I guessed right?" whispers I. "You are of the Basque race?" "Iberian, Domina," he says. "Close enough," says I. "I'm jolly good with Latin accents, actually," I says & hopes I'm not blushing too very much. "You are, like, our goddess, Domina," the girl says & prostrates herself, bowing down as though before Baal or some such sacrilegious iconography. "If you wish us," adds she, obsequiously, & looks up at me. "Wish you what?" says I, bored now & a-playing with them, impishly capricious & playacting somewhat, my mind redolent with stratagems & schemes, as per my perverse usual. Quite keen am I to mess with their tiny little minds/ brains: the young (& fetching) are so very easily fetched, as it were. "Should you, like, take us on, that is," says she in a very naïve voice, gullible & innocent. She's quite startlingly damnably pretty, the horrid, foreign, stunning creature. Gods damn her for a veritable charmer & exotic beauty. Shall I limn her, give you an expository picture? I shall. Clear light dreamy pale blue almond eyes, quite big & most engaging, & clean white teeth & fair hair & as I told you (five times now or so) great good high cheekbones—a lively visage, expressive & fresh. Such a fine, straight nose, as well—you could use it as a ruler—& smooth, creamy, tawny skin; touchable; it cries out somehow, it seems, for one to feel it. Pert, full breasts, pear-like, blanched peach-colored, ripe, plump, decolletagey. The boy—not so much, as in pretty: striking, handsome, nice straight teeth. She, though. She's so irremediably pulchritudinous in fact that I may have to scarify her a bit in case you, when & if you return, take a fancy to her. Scratch her across the face or perhaps have Cook hold with tongs a hot coal to her apple-like cheeks. That is, if I don't in abject frustration dismiss her first. Or have her "taken care of." She's the picture

of innocence—thus guilty as anything. I know her kind. I may just hie me
out to your armory & take a scimitar from your spoils box & put it not-
gently to her pink left cheek. Just the one. Just a nice long slash like a half
pink moon on her as I said *impossible* cheekbones (they're very high, but I
think I may have mentioned that) for her to remember me by as I watch
her flesh flower, the blood bloom as I watch in fascination, say, & the
wound rises like bread baking brown & golden-hued & honeyish. The red
blood pearls about her taut jaw & she recoils in horror & perhaps thrilling
libidinal excitation. Does my behavior seem odd somehow? My
intimations, I mean, my fantasies, hallucinations, etc.? I worry a slight bit,
I do. I wonder if I am with child, Caius? Would you welcome a third
bairn? I'm not so sure you would nor would I. Were I a man—& thank
my stars & trusty talismans that I am not, despite my hatred of effeminacy
of any sort!—I should want to do such things to her—our Laura—as I
know not how to put. She's quite dishy. Diabolically so, in fact. You know
how someone can be *too* beautiful? That's her. *Most* fetching. It's distressing.
Do you still find me attractive, Caius? I'm not asking out of vanity, but
from mere narcissism & genuine interest. I know I have put on some
weight since Julia. I know I'm vain. I know that. & I know you tell me all
the time how much you want me, love me, crave me, need me. But is that
just your julius talking? I do wonder, you know. It must be hard for you,
only having men, men, men around all day on tour. I mean, *I* wouldn't
mind that much! Hahaha! Only joking you, Caius. "One's too many & a
hundred's not enough"—isn't that what they say? Oh, that's about wine,
not men. My mistake. Similarly applies, though, don't you think? I do.
Now I think of it, I could do with a bit of "the grape" just about now.
I'll go clap for a glass & be right back... Okay, hail again. That's better.
So refreshing. Am so parched all the time. Thirsty. Yum! So good. Our
Roman winemakers really are the best in the world, don't you think. I
mean, I've never had glass nor goblet that's come from anywhere else, but
still? Can you imagine it—bloody Franks making vino? Or Spaniards?
Hahaha. Ludicrous. Anyway, I had better give this "other Laura" thing a

think. I'm most vexed right now, you've no idea. Well, some. How depressingly insecurely I have elevated her to "rival status." You know how haughty-envious I can be—you have seen it! Many-a-time, I shouldn't wonder. Another thing I wonder is whether Drusilla sent her so as to not have her in her (Drusilla's) own household, knowing full well what a little minx & temptress she'd easily turn out to be with the least bit of enthusiastic venereal encouragement, surely. Gods know Drusilla's husband's randy as a goat in heat & a big fat pig as well, outrageously unfaithful, an utter satyr—& everyone knows it. Makes nary an attempt to mask it, even. He'd make a pass at a plinth had it a vagina or a spare pair of breasts or puckered bumhole. He's a right shark if he's anything at all, that one. A proverbial wandering eye, the guy's got. As all men have, surely. Pigs & dogs all, every one. One could set all the men in the world in a line & saunter down it going "Pig, pig, dog, pig, dog, dog, dog..." till the end of time. Pigs &/or dogs, every one. Save you, of course, husband dearest. Were I personally the Sapphic type, a girl "from the Isle," as they say (of Lesbos, that is, in case you are too thick to catch the allusion, dear friend; a lesbian, in other words)—& I am most assuredly not from there; no way!—I'd have her, this new piece with the fatuous "brother," in my vast soft plush red bed in a trice. 'Twouldn't be so very hard to corrupt her & teach her the ways of the world. Hmmm. I wonder. Seriously now: in all candor, what the Hades should I do with these two? Not quite sure. I may take them on on an "on trial" sort of basis. Don't know, really. I so wish you were here to advise & counsel & chastise me. Read: spank me silly. Oh, Caius, you're so wise—in a sort of silly, duncelike, dum dum way. Hahaha. No, seriously—I mean it. Well, anyway. How d'ye do? What's new with you? You faring well & staying alive? Acquitting yourself on the gloriously vainglorious fields of superfluous battle? I hope so. Were you faring well, that'd make one of us, at least. I'm kerfuffled here; banjaxed to the max; I really really really have no idea how to do damage control on this whole Marius-killing-himself-thing. Everyone's aflutter. It's like some kind of nightmarish phantasmagoria round here. We're all like these oversized birds, flapping round, pecking at things, each other esp. Kids freaking, servants wailing. Word does travel fast: Aurelian came home from the field trip to Pompeii (with a lump of orangey lava rock as a sort of souvenir, I suppose; I hope he didn't spend too many denariuses on that nonsense; I mean, I could've sold him a stupid rock from our rock garden much cheaper, I'll warrant; bet you any money he doesn't even use it as a papyrusweight) & the first thing he asked was where neighbor Marius "did it," if you can believe that! He wanted me to show him; then he went round looking for all the blood stains! He wanted the servants to act it out for him like it was theatre! Mercury & Mars! Who bloody told him?! If I find out, someone's in for a disemboweling & a half. At the least a verbal one. I wish I had something pleasant & jolly to relate, convey, relay, impart. I don't, more's the pity. Still, I remain

Your (somewhat) faithful *Lora Caecillia*

XIII APRILLUS

Dear Friend:

Hail & let's forget for a moment about all pleasantries & formalities. & besides, the morning light's blinding me something terrible, if you know what I mean. It's got me in a mood most foul & pestilent, I've no doubt about that. Very in need of *et capillus de canis*, is what I am trying to say. Was most deep in my cups last night and oh if I'm not paying for it dearly now. Head's ponging like a out-of-tune gong. Apropos of how I signed off at the end of my last? Scratch that bit about "your (somewhat) faithful," I am sorry to tell you the new servant girl, whose name, as I think I related already, is also Lora, though she spells it wrongly: "Laura"—she & I fooled around a little bit this afternoon while the kids were down for a nap in the hot heat of midday. Damme, I don't know how or why that happened. Maybe the increasing temperatures had something to do with it. People *are* more amorous & frisky, they say, in warmer climes. On our honeymoon to the Amalfi Coast don't you remember how many times a day I wanted to "do it"? There—remember you wanted me to describe our wedding holiday? That should do for you. Ha! Anyhow, I am quite certain that it *is* getter hotter every twelve-moon that goes by. I wonder what the soothsayers would have to say about the heat rising in old Rome these days. Even though I don't care, I wonder what it's like in other cities as well, or if they say that more & more rivers & lakes dry up all over the known/mapped world. Anyway, Laura & I—I reckon it's just "something that happened," Caius, & I'm... I don't know what I am, really. I don't... *Is* it considered cheating when you're with— you know—someone who's of your same...? I mean, after all, you did have your own Grecian thing with that blasted camp boy. Just the once? & does that quote-unquote make you Greek? To have let him take your julius into his...I can't even write it! Okay: *mouth*. There, I said it. Or wrote it, rather. Same diff. I wonder now if, subconsciously, I may be trying to exact a bit of what they call *sweet revenge* here. Psychology, I believe they call it: when you do something equally heinous to your partner to get him back for the heinous thing he did, like letting a dirty-filthy & attractive Greek camp boy take your julius "just the one time" into his mouth. Egads, I am making myself mental here! Must stop. Must eat. Must drink. One sec. Be right back.... Okay, where was I? Perhaps the right & the wrong of this, the ethics (or morals?) will emerge if I just tell you what happened—or try to. My version & everything. Without too much sensationalism or embellishment or commentary & what you might deem a kind of insta-nostalgia. You know: a trumped up & salacious account like how the gossip papers they sell at the market talk. Well, talk

isn't the right word but you know what I'm saying. I am just so fuzzy (&
warm) right now so you'll have to pardon my Latin or what-you-will.
Okay: here goes nothing. A-dusting & a-watering the house plants, she
(Laura) had knocked a little vase over—not one of the antiques, but
something I was nevertheless quite partial to, the chalk-white, aquamarine,
& purple thing with capering revelers & horned, mythopoeic beasts.
Know the one I'm referring to? Good. It didn't even shatter—but it might
have done. Livid, I was. Plus excited as simply keening, just gasping for a
chance to upbraid, reproach, brickbat, etc. the young hussy or her so-
called brother. "Oh, this is nice! Most excellent handiwork! Bloody
clumsy child," says I, wonderly wroth, as you might expect; not happy at
her at all at all. "Come forth, imbecile thing," I, fulminating, says to the
stupid twat. She does. Comes she forth, within slapping distance. "Do
you realize what you have gone & almost done, klutz?" "No, Domina,"
says she. & so, to help her, show her, I cuffed her very very hard & she bled
at the mouth, the full brunt of my untrimmed nails finding then raking
red her olive-dough-fresh skin. "Forgive me, Domina," sobs she,
chuntering now, & blushing prettily. Well the red trickle from her plump
lips & the profuse and soft tears in her enormous eyes I daresay fairly
undid me & I told her quietly now: "Be still, you insolent little fool," & I
wiped the salt red blood from her fine chin & licked it (boy, did I ever wax
erotogenic at the sight of her fighting back tears, sobbing & pleading with
her big & kind & truly beautiful fuck-me eyes). Then I put my still-blood-
covered finger in her mouth—kissed her ever so softly, full flush on the
mouth, & lead her to my chambers. By the wrist—& so tight she bled
again. "Ow," she said. "You are, like, hurting me, Domina!"she said.
"Undress, whore!" I commanded. "You don't want to get blood on your
outfit now, do you?" I said. "& stop saying 'like' every flipping other word!
You sound like a cretin, talking like that, you, like, know? Like, *totally!*" Of
course it was a total ruse. She acquiesced, undressed. "Now—lay you
down, part your legs, & close your eyes," says I. "On your bed, Domina?"
she said, all small. "You wanna do it on the floor?" says me, & doubtless

a half-mast-eyed look of unmitigated concupiscence descends upon my thrilled & pleasure-anticipating visage. "I, I, I…" she charmingly stammers. "Are you a virgin?" asks I. "I think so," says the idiot. "If you mean…" "Shut up, you alien slut," says I. "What doth it matter? Lie back & let me taste you." Good gods was she ever sweet: just the right admixture of sweat & the juice of her, the way her *mons* foamed & the hot sweet liquid dripped down her "taint," & the half-moans & little cries of pleased surprise & clutchy "*oh-oh-oh*'s" from her pink mouth drove me half mad, I tell you. Afterward, as we lay back laughing the way one does post-coitus, sharing young figs & an opium pipe between us & giggling like naughty little girls, I very delicately & decorously asked her if she had ever felt such intense pleasure, in such a way. She gave a look askance like—as though searching for the right answer, as though I were asking her a trick question. Which (the look she gave) only meant of course that she had been gone down on so to speak before but didn't like to admit it lest I vainly flatter myself & assume I was her "first," as it were. So of course I up & slapped her again. Which admittedly rash action only pricked to the quick my enflamed desire redux & at we went it once more, this time with me a-sitting on her smiling-lovely lovey face, gyrating like one of the Furies, possessed. I call her "Spider." She calls me that, too. "Hello, Spider," I say to her. "Hello, Spider," she says right back & blushes & looks down & I brush her cheeks with the backs of my hands, left, right, back, forth. Why, I wonder, haven't we pet names for each other, you & I? It's a mystery. Quite, quite strange. I wonder if it means we… Well, I reckon we've been too busy with our respective busynesses to get round to it, pet-naming. Hm. If I send this missive—& that's a big, big if; I mean, I must be insane to confess this, tell you this, when the servants who heard & maybe watched are forbidden under pain of death to breathe a word of it, even if they're tortured on a rack or hung or hanged from their empurpled thumbs—I hope you will forgive me, dear. I was only carried away & merrily on the swift storm clouds of thundering lust. I wonder if we (you & I) didn't—you know—perhaps entangle/entwine our lives, get married too soon, too young, or if you were just... I'm only wondering here. Just a big heap of harmless hindsight, don't you know. Go on & arrow me verily through the heart of my heart if I'm out of bounds here but... I mean, gosh. You know how Pandora-like I am—wondering what "it" is like for men. Why else do you think I'm every once in a while pleading with you like anything to let me put the sheeny leathern stick I use for a you-know-what up your nice big Roman man-bum? & you never permit me to! Naughty Caius, naughty man. Let me reiterate—I don't want to *be* one, a man, that is (so many of my contemporaries, so many Roman women these days seem a bit resentful that they weren't born with a big, fat, hairy prick & a yen to go campaigning & subduing "infies" hither & yon, up hill & down dale, across the Tyrrhenian & the Adriatic; "It's a man's world & we only wait at home in it," they say & all that nonsense (stuff like, "This wouldn't have happened to me if I had a penis," or, "If only I weren't pregnant again" & all of that), but I do wish to understand their (your) sensibilities & sensations. & so I tried cunnilingus. Kill me &/or divorce me or have me poisoned or strangled if you wish to: I don't mind. Boil me in oil or a vat of bubbling fat; trip me & laugh long & loud as a stampede of livestock goes booming down our alleyway; club me over the head (from behind, grinning insanely) with a marble bust of mighty Hercules, as I am lifting my fair face to let the fat old sun shine upon it; on tippy-toes & snickering as you steal into my chamber while wearing a Grecian mask of some sort, cut my throat in my silken sleep; have me slowly disemboweled with a rusty trowel; plunge a dust mop down my gullet; bung me in with innumerable woebegone & greatly wailing Christians & have me thrown to the lions, tigers, panthers, hyenas, Jews, armed dwarves, mad bulls, etc.; force me at sword point off or heave me or have me hoved backward from a tall cliff above a veritable Charybdis or Scylla, or lower me (screaming, shrieking) into a pit of pythons, vipers, Cleopatras, or crocs; dunk me with a swift trip & without warning or a clean set of clothing into a dark, dank, dirty dungeon (is there any other kind? I mean, whoever heard of a nice, well-lit & spruced up hole-in-the-ground?); & lastly, take me to court & take me for everything I've got: I don't care.

Everybody's

entitled

to a

little

"experimental phase,"

& you know

I never

went

to college or anything, you know.

Cheers, then, from

Your little autodidact & poetess, *Lora Caecillia*

P.S. Well, not "your little"—who am I kidding?—but you know what I mean. I do miss you. Very. Nevertheless, why am I composing a post scriptum for a letter I will never post? People *are* strange. Even me.

P.P.S. In answer to your question re: snoring? Yes you do & you snore horribly, in fact. Why, aside from the fact that we are rich & can afford it, plus sometimes I can't stand the sight of you, esp. in the mornings, your puffy eyes, bad breath, starting-to-become-hairy back, etc., do you reckon we have separate bedrooms?

P.P.P.S. "Just sayin'." Haha.

XX APRILLUS

Dear Friend:

Hail. Let's see. What else to convey? Just got back from exercising at the gymnasium. (Yeah, right!) Bored out of my gourd—Drusilla's out of town, nobody's moved into Marius's old place, the warm spring sun enervates one relentlessly, the servants have informed me that no new books or tracts have come in to the book stalls in the market place, & the circuses & gladiatorial events have been temporarily shut down by the Senate for some reason or other, gods know why—I sat by yesterday & had some cups of wine from new goblets of bright blue glass. Laura, the girl servant I told you about, is such the resourceful little bargain huntress. I love sending her off to market with bit of ready money down her dress, love seeing what she ports back to add to the household! As I was saying, I sat by while Master Seneca did some extra one-on-one Socratic tutoring with your only son & heir. They were walking happily-contemplatively together round & round our simply-lovely-this-time-of-year courtyard, walking & talking, two gallants, one ancient, the other not. Your son & heir & his wise old tutor with his laurel crown of snow white hair & his beetling brows & his grotesquely efflorescent nose hairs, his donnish way of canting forward contemplatively, spotty white-gray hands clasped behind his markedly humped back. Those nose thistles make him look like he's sporting a bloody what-d'ye-callit—moustache! Unbelievably unmanly, that. An obscene thing if there ever was. Doesn't that sound majestic, though—your son & heir?! Aren't you blessed to have a boy, a son, Caius! At least I think he's yours! Kidding! He probably is. Seventy-five percent, maybe. We'll never know, though, won't we—on account of everyone says he looks way more like me than you. Lucky him! Ha! Any road, joking aside, I got a nice glimpse today of Aurelian's school world & his sedulous attempts to learn & deduce & reason aloud

& consequently shine. He's such a wondrous little prodigy—certainly the brightest in his class. By far. Much sharper, smarter, brighter, more curious & precocious than the III other little boys. One, a cretin, certainly, doesn't figure, but still; I think old Citizen Seneca keeps him under his tutelage in order to let the other lads practice kindness on the poor stupid bastard, the ridiculous eejit, drooling all over the texts & fisting clay into his mouth every chance he gets. Perhaps as a way to amuse myself & have a project, have something to do (gods, I'm bored—did I mention that? I have read everything ever written, it seems!) I'll render what I heard & witnessed as though it were an actual Socratic dialogue or—even better—a one-act play! Hark! Here goes:

SENECA Aurelian?

AURELIAN Yes, master?

SENECA Would you say, Aurelian, that wisdom was the greatest virtue?

AURELIAN I would.

SENECA & that we could call virtue good?

AURELIAN Yes.

SENECA *The* good?

AURELIAN Yes. I mean, I *think* so...

SENECA Good. & would you yourself like to be virtuous, as virtuous as could be?

AURELIAN Certainly.

SENECA & if you were to meet a wise & therefore virtuous man, would you not want to know how he came to acquire his wisdom?

AURELIAN What you say is doubtless true.

SENECA & what would you say to him?

AURELIAN (with furrowed brow) Um...

SENECA What might you *ask* him?

AURELIAN Could you repeat the question, please?

SENECA What would you ask him, in terms of finding out how he had acquired his wis...

AURELIAN Oh, um... I would say: "Tell me, sir: how did you acquire this wisdom of yours?"

SENECA Very good, Aurelian. Very, *very* good. Very well. Well then. Let us posit the notion that it would be good to meet a wise man, for he would be virtuous & good to meet.

AURELIAN Yes.

(Seneca here raising one brow & cocking his head, as if to ask "&?")

AURELIAN (faltering slightly, but recovering in time) Yes... um, in*deed?*

SENECA Absolutely. Very good. Wonderful, Aurelian.

AURELIAN (blushing) Thank you, revered Master Seneca Sir.

SENECA (wisely seeing that Aurelian was becoming a trifle fatigued, slumping a bit & dragging himself round the courtyard just a touch) Just a few more questions & then you can go & play for a short while—all right?

AURELIAN All right.

SENECA Let us now speak of politics.

AURELIAN Politics?

SENECA I ask the questions, Aurelian—you know that.

AURELIAN Oh, right. Sorry. You were saying?

SENECA That is another question, Aurelian—but never mind. Let's see now: & would it be also good for a *Senator* to be a good & wise & therefore virtuous man?

AURELIAN (seeing one of our dogs chasing a chicken across the yard, almost starting after; then with good discipline preventing himself from following an impulse) What? Oh, I mean: I'm sorry?

SENECA (closing his eyes meditatively, like a kind of aggravated Buddha) I said: '& would it also be good...'

AURELIAN Sure, sure, whatever.

SENECA (bristling, just a bit; stiffening perceivably) & would you like to become a Senator one day?

AURELIAN I would.

SENECA (smiling proudly, beaming my way, in fact) Because...?

AURELIAN Um, because no one could go round questioning me, Socratically. I could just do as I wanted. As I pleased, I mean. & because I could have *any*one tortured or poisoned or exiled or locked up in a...

SENECA Excellent. That's quite enough. Nice work, Aurelian.

AURELIAN (bowing a child's bow, a slight nod, as befits his higher-than-his-tutor station) Thank you, master.

SENECA Oh, don't mention it. You have done excellent well today, boy.

Run & play for a bit now & we will reconvene in half an hour & work on some Socratic questions concerning moral philosophy, then sums & sword fighting.

AURELIAN Thank you, master!

Aurelian wheeled & reeled around the fountain. I bought one with my own money & had it installed—my thought was, why wait for *you* to come home—if you even do? He was skipping round & round it, then, after spinning himself round & round in a dizzying circle, pretending with his little wooden sword to smite the servants, who had to "play dead" until he told them they could get up again. How he made me laugh as he told one of them "Arise! & receive our pardon!"—only to stab the poor sod soon as he (the poor sod) was getting up & was still on one knee. Clever little fellow, little trickster, little vamp! I had Laura's "brother" fetch my harp so that Julia could dance & sing & jump & amuse me. She has two or three special "moves" that, when she does them, make me smile & clap like crazy. The look on her precious face is so serious when she's performing them—like she's about to choke someone or run them through with a dagger or put a drop of poison in their Sunday punch. So precious. She gets this immensely cross look on her pretty little flower-face when I'm cackling at her & pointing at her like she's some kind of idiot. The look she gives is like she'd stab *me* through the thigh should she have half the chance. Maybe one day she *will*. Hahaha! When the break was up (the master went to the privy the entire time—& when he came out, breathless & looking flushed & thinner than ever, I asked after his digestion, if everything was "all right" & all that rot; I mentioned figs, prunes, etc.; he said he's tried everything; those only made him windy, poor chap; you aren't the only one who can't stand anything scatological: I fairly winced at myself for even mentioning the bog & for the hackneyed allusion to things "coming out all right;" just yuck!), old Seneca resumed his incontrovertibly brilliant teaching of our pride & joy, this time sitting at table with me. I think he needed to get off his feet after the colossal ordeal he must've underwent (undergone?) in the loo. Aurelian sat next to me so I could pet him & kiss him & run my anxious & doting & motherly digits through his hair while he learned.

The action picks back up in OUR COURTYARD:

SENECA To resume. Or you ready, Master Aurelian, to tackle &/or grapple with several questions concerning the philosophy of morality?

AURELIAN I am.

SENECA (conspiratorially) Let us know—I mean, now—speak of the traits, good or bad, of whole peoples. Who are the mightiest of all?

AURELIAN In terms of peoples?

SENECA Obviously.

AURELIAN We Romans.

SENECA & the bravest? Take your time, Aurelian.

AURELIAN Romans.

SENECA & you are quite sure?

AURELIAN Quite sure.

SENECA & the most beautiful?

AURELIAN (sighing) Romans—obviously.

SENECA The very same. Good, Aurelian. Most excellent work. Had I an ivory & purple ribbon upon my person I should garland you with it instanter. To continue: & superior to all other peoples the world over?

AURELIAN Romans!

SENECA Excellent. Superior, therefore, to Etruscans?

AURELIAN Yes.

SENECA Hebrews?

AURELIAN Very much.

SENECA Egyptians & Ephesians?

AURELIAN Naturally.

SENECA Visigoths, Franks, Athenians, & Ionians?

AURELIAN Yes, yes, yes, & yes.

SENECA Samaritans, Macedonians, Trojans, Persians, Dalmatians, & the thousand & seven assorted peoples of the land of Hind?

AURELIAN Definitely, Master.

SENECA & why?

AURELIAN (screwing up his pretty little face) Why?

SENECA Yes.

AURELIAN Because...um...because...

SENECA Yes! Just because. Excellent work, Aurelian. Your logic is impeccable. We Romans are superior because we *are* superior.

AURELIAN (with almost a sort cross look on his adorable little face) But, Master?

SENECA Yes?

AURELIAN I mean, isn't that something of a tautology? I mean...

ME (intervening) Master Seneca *said* you were right, Aurelian—what more do you wa...

AURELIAN (looking up with that look you know neither of us can resist) But I'm tired of all this Socratic questioning, mummy! May I have a snack, mummy? *Please, mummy?!* Please?! May I? Mummy!!

ME (interjecting, frowningly) Aurelian, you know snacks aren't good for you while you're learning. You must wait until it is snack time, until everyone has a snack—isn't that right, Master Seneca?

SENECA Well, he *could* maybe have a bit of fowl or cow—both are very good for the intellect. No bread, though. Bread is very bad for the...

ME (instantly clapping for Laura) Laura! Come hither, girl. Bring forth boiled cow & roasted fowl from the kitchen—for they are said to be good for the intellect! Order it from Cook. Wake her up if she's sleeping. She's always sleeping, Master Seneca. I think she overeats or something. Laura!

LAURA Right here, Domina.

ME Did you hear or should I say overhear what Master Seneca was...

LAURA Yes, Domina.

ME Well, then. A hefty plate of each—nice & thin-sliced like what we get from the marketplace! No bread, though. For bread is said to be bad for the intellect.

LAURA Yes, Domina.

ME & be sure, if it's not too much *trouble* for you, idiot girl, to bring forth a small hogshead of wine for us all—a very small hogshead... [Master Seneca shaking head here]...no, a very large one... For a repast without a companionable accompanying beverage is very bad for the intellect, is it not, Master Seneca? Very, very bad, is it not?

SENECA (smiling) Oh, *very* bad, Dame Lora Caecillia.

ME & for the soul?

SENECA Yes.

ME & for the digestion?

SENECA (sternly) Absolutely.

ME Little fool of a girl! Why are you standing there staring at me? Is there something wrong with my face? A bit of food in my teeth or an entire celery stalk or stick of carrot lodged in my hair?

LAURA No, Domina.

ME Are you laughing at me, impudent slut?!

LAURA No, Domina…it's just…

ME It's just what?

LAURA It's just that you're…

ME I'm what?!

LAURA Funny, Domina.

ME Funny ha-ha or funny…

LAURA Funny ha-ha, Your Highness.

ME Of course I am! Now—hurry along! & don't call me "Your Highness"! Who do you think I think I am—a queen?

LAURA Yes, Domina?

ME Yes?

LAURA No, Domina.

ME You don't think I could be mistaken for a queen—is that what you think?

LAURA I don't know, Spider... I mean Domina... I'm so, like, confused right now.

ME Leave us & fetch the tray of food for gods's sake! Spider? What can the girl mean?!

LAURA Right away, Domina. Forgive me, Domina. I was merely struck by your, like, hilariousness & loveliness, Domina.

ME You'll be struck by the palm of my hand if you don't get going. But thank you: that's very kind of you to say.

LAURA Yes, Domina.

ME But thank you, Laura. It's nice to have one's pulchritude appreciated— even by a low-born whore of a pretty little dirty servant girl.

LAURA Yes, Domina.

ME (brightly, to Seneca & Aurelian) Continue, continue...

SENECA Now, where were we?

AURELIAN Mummy, do you think Laura pretty, really?

ME (quizzically) Why do you ask, child?

AURELIAN *I* think she's pretty.

ME Oh, do you now?

AURELIAN I think she's very pretty.

ME (taken somewhat aback) Oh?

AURELIAN Yes indeed, mummy.

ME Do you fancy she's prettier than any of the other girls we have or have had?

AURELIAN Oh, very much so.

ME & do you fancy she's prettier than, say, someone like mysel...

SENECA Forgive me, Dame Lora, but...

ME Oh, of course.....you still have sums & sword fighting to get through today, plus a slight snack...

SENECA Thank you. I didn't mean to interrupt.

ME Never mind. 'Tis nothing. Proceed.

SENECA Now, Aurelian, where were we?

AURELIAN (sighing) Peoples...

ME Why do you sigh, Aurelian?

AURELIAN I'm tired of *answering*, mummy. I don't want to have to be so logical all the time! I'm just a boy, after all. Can't I go play, please? My mind hurts right now.

ME Hahaha! 'My mind hurts!' How very precious & precocious, don't you think, Master Seneca?

SENECA Doubtless it is so.

AURELIAN (squirmy, fidgety) Mummy, *please* may I...

SENECA Just a few more, Aurelian. All right?

AURELIAN I *guess* so...

SENECA There's a good lad. Let's see...would you ever trust an African? Ruminate judiciously.

AURELIAN Huh?

ME Just answer the question, Aurelian.

AURELIAN No.

SENECA No, you won't answer the question, or no you would not trust an African?

AURELIAN (sighing encore) Would not trust an African.

SENECA Excellent. Or borrow money from a Jew?

AURELIAN N...

SENECA (looking stern, looking cross) Um?

AURELIAN Yes?

SENECA Excellent. What kind of Jew would you borrow from?

AURELIAN I'm afraid I don't... Mummy, I...

ME Go ahead & answer, Aurelian.

AURELIAN A rich Jew?

SENECA Yes. &?

AURELIAN One I could trick somehow! Trip up in some devious way! Or slay for no reason! Maybe I could have him blinded so that he wouldn't, um, be able to see that I had tricked him into lending me money that I never would repay. & I would smite him if he even dared asked for terms!

ME Or?

AURELIAN Or...

SENECA (mouthing) *Mmm-mai...*

AURELIAN Maimed! I could have him maimed!

SENECA Precisely. Excellent!

AURELIAN So that he would not mind therefore the money not being repaideded [sic] but all his waking thoughts would be of his broken legs or severed arm!

SENECA *Most* excellent.

ME (clapping for joy this time) He really is quite a wonder, isn't he, Seneca? He's really coming along, is he not?

SENECA Oh, yes indeed. Great progress, we're making. Great strides.

AURELIAN Now can I please have something to munch? I'm *hung*ry, mamma. I haven't had anything at all to eat for over an hour now!

ME Be patient, Aurelian. & besides, here she comes with the plates now, the slut.

AURELIAN Goody!

LAURA (setting down a large blue & white marbled tray of boiled cow & roasted fowl) Your boiled cow & roasted fowl, Domina.

SENECA Just one more enquiry before we break. This cult you may have heard about of late—the Christians—say in their ecumenical way that their curious & strange god teaches them that they must, and I quote, "turn the other cheek" when slapped by an assailant. That is their teaching. What do you make of *that*, Aurelian?!

AURELIAN Hahahaha!

SENECA I *know!* Incredible, huh?!

ME Hahahaha! Priceless. Do they really? How *very* strange & curious! Where do they *get* this stuff from, I wonder?

SENECA Seriously. So what would you do, should someone strike your cheek, Aurelian? Would you turn the other toward him & permit him to…?

AURELIAN Certainly not! Are you kidding, Master S? I mean…

SENECA (breathlessly, really swept up in his outstanding pedagogy, nodding his encouragement of our brilliant son) What should you do?

AURELIAN Strike *his* cheek!

SENECA Or…?

AURELIAN Or…?

SENECA Or…? Think hard, Aurelian.

AURELIAN Poison him—if I could.

SENECA Or…?

AURELIAN (pantomiming stabbing) Run him through with my sword!

SENECA Or…?

AURELIAN (whinging) *I* don't know. I'm tired of all this poisoning & stabbing & striking inferior peoples. It's fatiguing, surely. Mummy! *Please* can we eat now, please?

ME Aurelian, you know you must ask Master Seneca...

AURELIAN Master Seneca, can we...oh but he's already got a handful of cow or owl in his mouth, mummy.

ME Master Seneca! Wait—owl? Are we eating owl here, Laura?! I said fowl, not owl!!! Laura!

LAURA Yes, Domina?

ME This is not owl—is it?

LAURA I don't know, Domina!

ME Well, whatever it is, Master Seneca, you should *not* have begun eating first!

SENECA Sorry, Dame Lora Caecilia. Forgive me. I work up such an appetite, teaching. You're not the only one, Aurelian.

ME (indulgently) All right, my dears. Let's all partake. Fetch the bloody wine now, Laura.

LAURA Yes, Domina.

Exit LAURA, we THREE eat with great relish and bonhomie. End Scene.

So you see how quotidian Roman life continues apace in your absence, Caius. I brought my leathern writing pad & scroll out to the courtyard to be a sort of stenographer for you so that you could feel somehow like you were there, like you were here with us, watching Aurelian shine. & I hope you have enjoyed this little vignette about how we're faring. I do wish you would come home soon, but I am content with the children & watching them grow. You're the one I feel sorry for, despite my occasional ennui & despair & the intermittent desire to put an end to myself with a dull knife (kidding!): you're missing out on so much, la. Before you know it, Julia will be happily married (if she doesn't turn out a courtesan like those jades your sisters), & Aurelian a great, saturnine statesman or popular local tyrant. Please get all the killing, smiting, warring, etc. you can over & done with & come home to me (with open arms & legs),

Your Lora Caecillia

P.S. Too peevish right now to write a P.S. Frustrated, Caius. Randy. Damn this damnable state of affairs.

P.P.S. Oh, Caius, Caius! This is horrible, just horrible. Something terrible's happening. Seneca's dying. I'm not kidding around, either. He's sitting here across from me choking on some colorful candied almonds (I don't know why they call them *Jordan* when they're made in Italy at any number of confectioners right here in our borough or near it at least) Laura brought out after we feasted on a bit more cow & some suckling pig, post-sword fighting & sums lessons. Such a potpourri of pretty pastels, those pretty-colored candies—yellow, blue, pale brown, purple, pink, and white. Delicious! & you know how I love them. The dish being offered him, Seneca smirked & said "I really shouldn't," but urged him to indulge, a.k.a. why not, go ahead, help yourself, live a little, you've questioned Aurelian so relentlessly today, worked so hard, spoil yourself, you deserve a tasty treat, you only live once, etc.; & he says "All right, okay" & his well-veined & hoary-hairy hand sort of hovers whitely over the rich mélange of happy candies & he laughs a bit of a plosive laugh & breathes in that noisome whistling way most oldsters have, & finally he takes an handful (no modest or decorous amount, at all), a real jumble of them & starts flicking a mess of them into his big old gob & before you know it *he's holding his wizened throat & writhing round & gyrating & making a sound like a hundred chickens make when a fox or mingy old raccoon's got into the hen house*; & Julia (who's just woken up from another nap, & who is sitting on my lap) just starts shrieking & Aurelian tries slapping the dear old soul on the back with his (Aurelian's) little painted wooden sword (the silver & gold one with the gold & scarlet tassels—so adorable, that one) & he's not *not* breathing quite yet (Seneca, that is, not Aurelian, thank Aeolus), but as I write this (oh no, Caius!) the dear old dotty worthy's turning all shades of purplish red & bright blue & I'm furiously trying to finish this seemingly interminable (& seemingly impossible to terminate) sentence & instead of doing something, bustling about on their better's behalf or at the very least sending haste post haste for a surgeon or an apothecary, the stupid servants are just standing there, positively flipping out & covering their spastic mouths with their red-raw & fluttering, pusillanimous hands & at last he (Seneca, the silly old dodgy old fool) keens then keels over horribly, onto the courtyard tiles (I got a sweet deal on them—the men who put the fountain in did them in half a day, I think), & his appalling pink tongue jets out with a mishmash of masticated candied almonds frosting it, coating it, for gods's sake, & his scary-great green eyes bug like the dickens. "Mastwer Senecwa, Mastwer Senecwa!" Julia's shouting & pogoing now like anything. "Don't *shout* so, Julia," I'm going. "Try & be a little ladylike here, all right?" "But, mummy," Aurelian goes, "he's not *breathing*, mummy." "Oh, for gods's sake," I say. They can be such drama kings & queens sometimes, your kids. "Of course someone's not going to breathe when they're choking to death on something, you silly goose—especially when the something they're choking to death on's got a hard candy shell! Oh blast & bother—what a pother! Hang on a sec," I say & I put my pen down & go over & I grab Julia & set her on the old boy's chest & I go "Jump, Julia, jump!" & she gives me a too-frank look like, "But you're always telling me *not* to jump, mummy," & I give her a look in turn like, "It's okay; forget about all those other times: do you reckon you can do me a favor just this once & jump on an old man's choking chest for me?" & wouldn't you know it but after five or six good hard thumping leapings up & landings down on sweet little precious Julia's part (it took her a couple of tentative practice ones, jumps, that is, to really get going & throw her adorable little arms into it & catch some serious air & *put* some air therefore *into* old Seneca), a mess of candy shrapnel comes foaming out the old trout's mouth & he's alive & kicking & I, your quick-thinking & really quite clever & industrious humble servant (well, not a servant, but you know what I mean), have saved an important man's life, a philosopher's life no less, that of a demigod or potentially deified person—if he ever gets it together as a writer, that is, & comes out with a smash hit of a bestseller, something for the lay person who's interested in philosophy, logic, sums, Roman supremacy, & sword fighting. Well, anyway—how d'ye like that?! Ha! Haha! Hahahaha! You know how I hate to blow my own trumpet, but, by golly & by gosh & without any unseemly fanfare & ceremony—pretty nifty wife you've got there, Mr. Bigshot Legionary Caius Aquilla, wouldn't you say? A sort of a modern superheroine, an almost-goddess, & a near-legendary example to all Roman women kind, surely. If I do say so myself, in all immodesty.

P.P.P.S. Long dramatic & to say the least draining day today so I think I'll have just one more nice fat goblet of red, then some white, then set sail for dreamland. Hope you are well. & alive of course. Mwah!

XXI APRILLUS

Dear Friend:

Hail. Well, well, well: the inevitable. Laura & her "brother" are no brother & sister at all, but brazen, horrid, twofaced, clandestine lovers. Ha! I knew it. The silly sneaks! So vexed. Color me a woman betrayed. This is an outrage & a most maddening one! Here's how they are discovered, & thus undone. No sympathy of any kind have I, for one, for them. Not being able to sleep, I rose in the middle of the night & put on my blue & sparkly silver satin slippers & my favorite sheer robe of flowing royal purple & went to look at the moon, that glorious orb, symbol of mutability, or at least check to see if there was one on account of I couldn't remember if there was one or not & oh by Diana if I didn't through the slats of the servants' quarters spy Laura & her golden-curly-haired sham & of an hirsute "brother" a-nuzzling & a-spooning & a-holding each other as tight & fast & close as the night is long! They looked so peaceful & content & innocent it made me want the vomitorium on an empty stomach! I can't believe I was so very duped! & yet not: I suspected them all along—I will say that. Ready to scratch their eyes out was I! When confronted (I took off one slipper & threw it at them from a very short distance as a way of telling them physically that I was no fool & now fully on to their sordid-salacious scammy scheme), their olive skin went in tandem the color of milk pudding or tapioca & like adolescent ghosts & in great confusion they hopped to their dirty-disgusting flat & grotesque peasant feet & stammered worse than Marius (poor dead Marius) ever did. "What is it, Domina?" the fool of a boy, rattled, prattled. "Keep your voice down, imbecile!" said I in my of course inimitably minatory way. "You'll wake the entire household, you ridiculously imbecilic flibbertigibbet, oaf, & rube!""What is it, Domina?" he said at just the same volume, but an octave lower, the cretinous wretch. "What have you done? What have you done? Why, gods damn you both to Hades, you're lovers, not sister & brother!" said I, rhymingly. "We were, uh, only, um, like, keeping one another warm, Domina!" Laura pleaded & got down on her knees & held up pathetically praying hands, then lifted her inestimably pretty, duplicitous, & tear-streamed face to me. "Like, for sure," the blithering-shivering boy says. "Oh fa-la-la!" said I, "'brother' indeed! Fiddlesticks, fie, & fiddle-dee-dee!" "Huh?" the boy says, but never mind him. In a wax, I says to her, the girl: "If that is so—& it is decidedly not!—then you have committed incest with him, your 'brother.'" "Indeed we have not, Domina," the meretricious little bitch says. "Please listen," pleads the stupid lad. "Liar!" says I, & slapped her a right quick good one, the sound of the blow I'd struck I'd liken to the report of a well-tuned tin drum like the one Aurelian rat-a-tat-tats on once in a while (isn't he just adorable?). It wasn't, the slap I slapped her, that hard, in other words (she's such a baby sometimes, you know?). She wimpered. I laughed. My laughter reminded me I should focus & wax indignant, wax cruel, put my foot down as they wax lachrymose, wax penitent, pathetic as a to-the-lions-thrown Christian or Jew: "D'you expect me to believe such codswallop, hussy? It makes for sixty-seven Celsius out here if it's one degree at all! It's warmer than my admittedly quite fiery temper, it is! You're lovers! Admit it! I saw you! I'll brook no denial here." "I don't, like, understand you, Dom…" says the girl. I go: "Lookee here: you've been having each other the entire time you've been in my employ, you nasty-randy horrid filthy dirty attractive foreign creatures! Rutting like mad, like anything. You know you have! The truth! Out with it! If there's one thing I cannot take it's lies. Lies, lies, lies!" My attempts to gorgonize the appalling two of them go for nought: "No, no, no, exalted Domina," they squealed in barbarous chorus, & the boy drops dramatically to his golden brown servile knees & folds his dumb, illiterate hands like he's praying to Venus & Juno together. Just then I noticed they've matching & contrapuntal open sores on their upper lips—kisses from Eros, presumably. Bah! Revolting! What utter shamelessness. And just then I began to wonder if they often rehearsed together this sort of stuff, this posturing & madly phony supplicating, when they're alone. What utter twaddle. What cheek. What acting! & you know how I despise pretense & thespianism more than anything, more than weakness, more than vegetables! Never thought them capable of such chthonic, bathetic depths. "It is not so," the boy says lamely, as though he's speaking Latin for the very first time, querulously, creepily, obnoxiously, nauseatingly. I reckon he thinks he sounds convincing & sincere, pious & penitent, believable. Ha! Ha, ha! No dice. Not a chance. Suchlike rebarbative groveling only makes me detest & wish to thrash & thrash him more & more. Hypocrites, both of them! Oddly, in the midst of this I realized that all this drama & strife is making me feel peckish; I nearly go ordering them into the kitchen to make me a snack so that I can refresh myself before we resume. But I don't, figuring they might abscond or giggle together & talk about me, or poison me somehow or put a hot pepper in with some cow & bread or something, for cod, the little imps & gorgeous scalawags. "Why do you talk like a demented baby?" I asks him. "Your beauty blinds me, Domina," says he, appealing & quite successfully, I might add, to my vanity. Why is it, I wonder, that we forgive that rote fault in a woman & readily, but in a man it is most unwelcome, effeminate, & revolting? It is a vice & a fault like any other; yet female conceit's tolerated if not encouraged. What did we give little Julia for her fourth birthday last—do you remember? I'll tell you: perfumes, a looking glass, hairbrushes encrusted with opals & rubies. "Well..." I say & must have blushed a bit. "I *am* said to be...accounted to be...renown, actually, to be..." "As beautiful as the biggest star in the sky," the brazen boy bellows boldly. "The biggest star?" I, incredulous, blurt out & cock my eye in a most forbidding way, dead at him. "You're saying I'm *heavy*, I'm big as a *star*?" "No, no, Domina," he blunders. "Gods damn you both," I say. "That was not my meaning," says he. "Liar!" I says. "D'you reckon I'm in any mood to bandy words with you, sirrah" "I didn't mean that!" he said. "He didn't," cries she. I give them both a look that announces that I don't believe them for an instant. "Truly, Domina," Laura supplicates & looks at me with those almond doe-eyes of beautiful blue so blue they sparkle in the dark, they do. I know I am often "deep in my cups," as they say; ineffably bibulous; everyone who knows me knows that. But do they (these "siblings") deign to think, I wonder, that I was born yesterday & not yet weaned? "Lie a-down again," I says, barks quietly, that is. They do. "Turn over!" "Yes, Domina," they says. "Remove your cheap-o togas first!" I says. "What?" the idiot boy says. Again!? Has he learned no manners of me, serving me? Is he deaf? Kids these days—their *modi operandi* boggle the mind, Caius, I'm telling you. "You incorrigible bastard," I says. "Lie down face down, completely naked!" I says. "I'm not sure that's a good idea, Domina," the cheeky boy says. "I have trouble breathing unless I'm lying on my…" "You impossible imp," I say, as they both have wild, animal looks in their eyes and icicle smiles going— exceedingly provocative, "here you are offering your utterly valueless opinion when I have found you out—spooning like honeymooners, in moonlight no less." "We were just, like…" Laura proffers. "Cease!" I say. "Don't you know that Hades hath no fury like a woman scorned? You dunces! Now: off with your kits!" Off go their kits. I squeeze in & kneel between them, triumphing internally. It isn't difficult, me making room for meself upon the sordid bed—they're way on opposite sides of the kip space that's supposed to be just for the girl. Quivering like oysters now. I go: "Now: this is for your own goods, you reprobates & mendacious barbarian n'er-do-wells," & I begin to run my long sharp hard mahogany nails full deep, lifting my bum up & getting some deal of nice torque from my legs so that I can really dig in, score their bare & exposed & creamy backs. "You'll like this," I say, breathless, expectant, indeed aroused. "You'll take this & like this! Now… There! How do you like that?! Doesn't that feel good, children?" I say rhetorically of course & I continue to make them both squirm like mad & say "ow!" & "Please, Domina!" & all that rubbish & as I scratch & scratch like a cat trapped in a box or two lust-crazed women fighting over a handsome, priapic gladiator who can't run away on account of he's lost one leg to a tiger or lion, as I nail them as it were, like anything, they sort of start to turn round in pleasant pain, their fucked, voluptuous faces begging for mercy in the blue light of the chamber & for me not to stop, not to desist from hurting them horribly, wonderfully; & I kiss better, metaphorically speaking, the skin where the red's raised up & left a hard mark. The salt red blood curdles forth in rennels & I trace a star on the back of the wench, then run my hands in tandem along their young taut pert fine round bums & working thighs & fine waists & I kiss Laura's proffered neck (then bite it, softly, softly!) & so-fine hair & pull the boy's exceedingly tumbleweedy mop (& bite him, his head—I don't even know his dumb stupid name; I just call him "Boy!") & I clutch the little whore, the little liar & minx, by her wettening crotch & I begin to finger her gently-sweetly & gingerly & teasingly from behind as I yank the lad's jules out & down at the same time like cook stirring a batter with a stirring stick & they turn to me both as if to beg & plead for their lives or at least their privates & I kiss one of them, one then the other (not on their pox-marked lips, natch) &, in fine, they look up now with ass-kissy eyes & we proceed to have a threesome or three-way or orgy or *ménage-a-trois* or whatever the Hades you call it. Hang them both for a pair of slattern sluts. Afterward, after he fucks me & I come, & I fuck him & he comes, & I fuck her & she & I both come, & I fuck her while he watches & frets like a great baby, then she licks me while I suck his fat little stub of a barbarian cock...as we daisy chain away & it all goes round & round. Afterward, I slap good & hard both of their faces blue, hard as I can in light of my "spent" state; & I go back, pad back, to bed & tell them I will deal with them in first thing in the morning or at least by noon. Seriously resisted the urge to wake Cook up and have her make me an individual pizza with everything (hope you are proud of me for practicing self-restraint!). With love from your very cheesed-off & chagrined to find I have been hoodwinked so, so gulled; bamboozled, as well,

Lora Caecillia

P.S. If perchance I send this preposterous missive by mistake—if it gets in the post by accident somehow—know that I am in the midst of writing *My First Imaginary History*, husband dear. Isn't that exciting?! Yes, exactly! I think that's the right term for it—Imaginary History! How novel of me! How clever I am. In other words, I've made stuff up. I'm so bored—colossally so—& that's why I write all this stuff & nonsense. Writing made-up stuff's just a way to make me not feel so lonely while you're away. At least I can be with my characters, my puppets, if I can't be with you, dear friend, dear love. None of this sexy stuff actually happened, is what I am trying to say. Or did it? Ha! (Wink, wink.) Now you don't know what to think, eh? Okay, fine. It's all a lark, fabricated. Perhaps. Ha, again! Look: modern erotica (with a twist—though I'm not sure what that twist might entail) might be my literary métier & I am trying out a voice here & there. You know what a big fan I am of both Catullus & Sappho; it's just that I don't feel like a poet; I don't think I could write it really, so I spin my yarns in epistles like this one. & my prodigious libido (not to mention my equally-wicked-as-yours sense of humor) seeps in to my inky plume, me thinks! What do you think? Of the scene I've just scribbled? Tell me. Be honest—as long as you think it's brilliant & fine & among the most beautifully crafted & triumphantly artistic & affecting love scenes you've ever read.

XXII APRILLUS

Dear Friend:

The kids are both dead, a double suicide. They were found in the girl's bed, holding hands, their mouths blackened with poison. The servants have set up a dreadful hue & cry. I don't know what to say save a most sorrowful hail from

Your Simply Devastated

Lora Caecillia

XXII APRILLUS

Dear Friend:

Dear gods just as the post-fellow made away away & down the lane I realized that in my last I wrote something frightfully ambiguous & easily misleading, startlingly misleading, eminently misinterpretable, etc., & it hit me that you might think that by "the kids" I meant our Aurelian & Julia! Oh, no, no, no, no! What I should have said was the servant girl I was telling you about, Laura, & her "brother" were found this morning, their mouths filled & faces blacked with tarlike poison. In my startled state & grief-stricken one as well I didn't edit too well. I sent one of the surviving servants a-running after the damned post-fellow, to stop my last, but to no avail. Telling ya: he's fleet as bloody Mercury sometimes, that guy, darting down a lane, up an alley, over an aqueduct, through a tunnel, into one of the public gardens, shortcutting through an abattoir, leaping from one second story house to the next, skipping through a walkway, a thoroughfare or byway, nipping up a long flight of stone steps. It's no good trying to tail or trail him now; & waiting down the Central Imperial Roman Post Office to try & intercept the letter won't do any good as they all look alike anyway, those post-fellows, with their bald pates & leathern bags; & once your letter's in the hands of the Central, well, you'd best forget about it: the forms you've got to fill out, the red tape & bureaucracy, the runaround & papyruswork & possible animals you have to bring in for offering—not a jot worth it, let me tell you. Damn it all! My only recourse is to write haste post haste this follow-up to tell you to discard my mine of XXII Aprillus if you get it, &/or hope that the Roman mail's intercepted on its way to you this time & the civil servants who deliver your letters are ambushed & slain by Visigoths or Germans or something & all letters (esp. mine) scattered to the Four Winds. I've quite simply got, got, got to stop writing you when I'm plowed. Thing is, I *like* writing wasted, toasted, wrecked, smashed. There's something…thrilling about it. Reckless & quite deliciously stupid! Nevertheless. Write drunk, edit sober, is what I always say. So (as this is serious now; serious business) let me reiterate & pray that *this* letter actually gets through to you (& I think I will, just for insurance's sake, sacrifice a bird of prey today, a baby owl or grotesque kite) & the other does not. How slippery is language & Latin especially. Oh this never would have happened had I been allowed to be formally educated, take a few writing classes; that way, I'd've learned to edit meself, take out the vestigal bits, revise the stuff that could be taken wrongly. *Viz.*, what I just said. *Ibid.* etc. We autodidacts have it rough, don't you think? All this fretting & worrisome concern has made me sport-eat like mad, sorry to report: I just downed an entire roast chicken with boysenberry icing, & a heaping pyramid of white chocolate fudge, also with boysenberry icing (Cook's used it on everything today—I think she made too big a batch). Well, that's all, really. Nothing much more to add, I don't think. Remind me to look up the word "panjandrum;" I came across it in my reading t'other night & was too tipsy to get up from the fainting couch where I reclined to consult a dictionary. What a funny-funny word. I must know its meaning. Anyway & sweet goodnight from

Your Lora C.

P.S. Oh dash it all—I couldn't sleep for not knowing that word! So I got up & fetched the dictionary from the dusty old library (nobody goes in, now you're not here to putter round it). Here's what I found. "Panjandrum"=one who has great knowledge or expertise in something. Used in an original sentence: "'I am panjandrum of nothing,' said the lonely Roman housewife whose husband, away at war, has left her far too long alone." There's a sentence for you. For you to stick in your bally craw or your silly helmet, valiant absent warrior.

P.P.S. Can't take this much longer, much more of you being away, by the way. I'm so lonely I could scream.

P.P.P.S. Just screamed. Didn't help one bit. Only made me feel even more lonely. Lonely, lonely, lonely.

XX APRILLUS

Dear Friend:

Hail. Today we had off, no attacks or recons or dangerous sweep-and-clears; hence everyone in mufti and football, football, football is the thing on almost everyone's mind and agenda; that alone. Morning, noon, afternoon, and even early evening—footie it is, was, shall be. What a boring sport! I know it's "universal" and everyone goes mad for it, but for Hermes' sake, how utterly uninteresting a contest it is if you can't use your hands, the *dexter* and *sinister* tools the gods gave you to serve and protect you. Imagine a fray without hands—a bunch of legless blighters fighting each other with their *feet*?! Ridiculous! Hardly manly. Football! It's a *mania*, I tell you. Here's my report on the so-called action: Play begins. Our ball. Brutus passes it over to Joc, pats it to Lt. Optio, Optio dribbling like a fiend, poncily showing off, dancing a merry jig back and forth while everyone else falls asleep or merely stands there with arms dangling or goes to Crete or Sicily or Firenze in their tiny little minds, Optio gooning, overdribbling, his fine black hair in a thin headband, the locks behind the headband peacocking prettily on his bobbing head, juking, jinking, jibing, jiving, reversing field, ball-hogging his merry little way down the proverbial lane or, neologistically, cobblestone street, now looking like chimp, now like a Pict doing the sword dance they do with the crossed swords and the hands high in the air all dandyish, now looking like someone who's been stabbed (repeatedly) in the face. Optio, I say, gets it (the ball) stolen by the other side (big deal!), Joc steps in and dives feet first and thumps it "dramatically" away from a guy on the other team. Time out. Halt of play. I must say Joc looks great without a tunic; we all do, in fact. In again. Joc jumps up, sort of somersaults, chases it, chases it, chases it (yawn!), trips and falls, supinely stretches for it (the ball), then accidentally toes it out of bounds. Opposition's possession. Their ball. We've been at this idiocy for twenty or thirty minutes and no one's been carried off with a compound fracture, broken shin, or a gushing head wound. Boring! Boring, boring, boring. Okay. Play continues. There I am: I intercept the inbound pass from the guy on the other team, catching it in my crotch, but then I kick it out of bounds—having swung with my leg and missed it, but kicked in the julius a bloke on the other squad. My mistake. My bad. Sorry about that, mate. "Are you all right?" I asks him, him moaning and writhing on the ground and grabbing his nuts. It's positively awful seeing anyone like that, plus totally hilarious! I can't stop larfing. The "universal" nine people—spectators—looking on go: "Boo! Boo! Foul play! Hissssssss!" I shrug. The umpire or referee or what-d'ye-callit's whistling like mad and wheezing like he's going to keel over any minute: he's looking extra chubby in his cumbersome waistcoat of zebra skin or impala hide or whatever. He holds up a yellow card. What's he doing with a playing card on his person? Are people betting on this foolishness? What fools! An inbound pass from one on their side to one on their side, then Brutus slyly slides in, darts in like an orange human arrow and pokes the ball (the wrapped-in-burlap human head) desperately with his instep, pokes it over to Joc, Joc taps it to me, me (miraculous surprise!) to dear swift Brutus on a clear and reckless breakaway, B bursts all crazylegging past a defender, then another one, running like a drunken thief in the night, and then he heels it back to trailing-sprinting Joc who desperately crosskicks it *wide* of the fisherman's net set up as goal between two branches plunged into the grass and mud and much of whichever country we're in. "*Ohhhhhhhhhhh,*" goes the little crowd of camp boys, cooks, and slaves looking on. "Yawnnnnnnn," goes me who is one of the players, no less! I can't believe how popular this stupid nonsense is! A gaggle of little school girls in their best dresses and with garlands in their hair and teacups in their hands could play this game, this "beautiful game," as enthusiasts dub it. Ha! What's so pretty about a bunch of sweaty Roman men running after and vying to kick a severed barbarian head wrapped in a burlap sack, eh? And as for the onlookers, the ones who care (and there are many, so many the world round, I'm told), there's such suspense for them, they say! Nothing compares, they say. Had they half the chance they'd do nothing all the livelong day but watch football, bet on football, talk about football, hear the town criers cry the daily football report, read about football in *The Daily Papyrus* or the sport section of *The Eternal City Journal of News, Gossip, Foreign Domination, & Slaughter*. What for?! I just don't get it. How we Romans could have thunk up this dreck *and* at the same time have conceived of the glorious and mind you *truly* nail-bitingly exciting sports that take place in the gladiatorial rings boggles the proverbial, it does. It boggles the very. Have I not many-a-time wanted to go over to them, the people on the sidelines, the punters, and to say to them, "You never seen a Frank's or Pict's head kicked round a grass plot or poxy sandbox?! This your first time or somefink? You look like you're seeing a volcano explode or a brutal crucifixion! What's the deal with you people? For gods's sake, go do some light reading or trim your fingernails—*anything* but watch this silly silliness!" The generals are smarter than that. The generals, the glorious and illustrious generals, can't be arsed to gaze on from the tumulose landscape they perch on, look down from: eminences looking down at/on us from an eminence! Hahaha! Nice pun, eh, Lora? I know: not that good. Sort of a cheap riff. I can do better. I know I can. It's just that I'm tired. So very. The generals: they might be up there looking but they're not watching, they're too busy to do so anyway—rumor is they're mostly concentrating on palavering amongst themselves, trading compliments, and munching on the afternoon tea the cooks have specially fashioned for them: gooseberry tarts and roasted duck-on-a-stick, dipped in—yes, you guessed it—raspberry sauce, baked cinnamon and brown sugar cane apples, and tea with goats' cream and a swizzle stick of baby sugar cane apiece. I fairly drooled, hearing what they've been getting for tiffin and tea of late and seeing them (from a distance, of course) in their camp chairs and wrapped up in snug fox or mink rugs for the rainy mists that swan in then lift intermittently then dissipate unpredictably as we hoof it up and down the makeshift pitch. How I wish someone would invent a game where, if it rained, everyone went inside and had a nice cup of Earl Grey and perhaps some strawberries and cream, a jam butty, some tuna sandwiches, then an ale! A game, a real *sport*, where there was a net, say, and one's opponent was on the other side of it! Playing football, I keep getting kicked in the shin (sometimes left, most times right) by some fit oaf with dark hair and chiseled cheekbones above a headband rag of sea-purple and white and red (the Legion's "team colors"). Why couldn't there be a legitimate sport where two opponents patted a softish but still quite bouncy and hard pink, white, or yellow (for maximum visibility's sake) ball, say, back and forth on a lined court, a rectangle on clay or tar or grass—a field of actual, demonstrable beauty: something dark green, bright blue, or light red. The two or perhaps four players would pat or bat the ball till one of them either hit the damn thing beyond a baseline or past his flailing adversary for a "winner"! What a game that would be! The weapons the foes might employ to hit the ball could be made of wood, and something like a net or flattened basket themselves, an oversized webbed spoon, say, or dried gut of cat, in string form perhaps, stretched across to make a sort of fibered or filaments-oriented bat! And women could play as well and not be thought butch or Dutch. Women playing! How could that not be beautiful—and elegant. Like dancing and competing at the same time! I envision everyone in yellow, perhaps. No! Wearing light blue! Or all-white—yes, that's the ticket. Softest lambs' wool. With little insignium of a devil's horn or a mini-crocodile on their shirtsleeves. And the ball made of coarse yarn spun from the finest Roman wool. The championships once a year in the sun-dappled Coliseum—the winners gathered from other tournaments held regionally. Perhaps four major ones: Rome (of course; the championship of championships), Alexandria, and, um, two others To Be Determined. Brilliant! Carthage, maybe? Athens? I really think I have alighted upon something here, dear friend! What to call it, though?! It's got to have a catchy name or it won't catch on—knowing the fickle and unimaginative Roman sporting public. Netsy? Shuffleswitch? Bouncepatball? Something will come to me. I'll come up with something. What do you think, Lora? Aren't you marveling right now—at your husband, I hope?! He's just invented a sport! Wholly in his mind! Quite a fellow, quite a chap, wouldn't you say? Oh, you'd probably poke holes in it, my imaginary game—find some way to say, "You silly ass—who'd play such a bloodless thing?" I'm going to work on it some more and...what to do? Petition a senator somehow to start up a league? Do it informally? But where? And how? Oops, gotta go now, the horns have blown for mess: tea, bison, and a salted, pan-fried biscuit. Big effing deal. Not even a spot of olive oil to drip on it, the biscuit. Things are bleak these drag-along soldiering days, dear friend. Longing for home, your arms, my bed, the kids, the animals, and a goat cheese pizza. I want pizza so bad right now, dear friend: we drag everything off via wagon whilst campaigning, you know—why not a wood-fired pizza oven: makes no sense!—more than ever is

Your Caius Aquilla

P.S. On the sidelines, near a line of cypress trees and just the bluest hydrangeas, as I was "taking a knee," a break and breather, Brutus (you know, the excessively orange-hued, dashing-handsome Q'master) and I got to talking while two other blokes subbed in for us, trotting in like thoroughbreds, like thoroughbreds with their arms held out like kangaroo arms—hence thoroughbred kangas. Things got a bit political, rather, in terms of our chat, Brutus's and mine. Politics—which as you know aren't or isn't my forte but sometimes I get to wondering about. . .stuff like that. Political stuff and that. Not that I know much about it. It's all Greek to me really, but I do have my opinions, however shaky, however tendentious, biased, Rome-centric, jingoistic, xenophobic, and correct—the full party line. It isn't all just jibes and yucks with me, don't you know. I can be serious, lugubrious, atrabilious. What true poet is not, sometimes. And I am a poet at heart, I know I am. All I must needs do is begin to produce poems and *voila!* my destiny will be mine. Poems and a five-to-ten minute one-man show bit, that's all. Now to the issue at hand: of course soldiers of any rank aren't of course supposed to question foreign policy and all that rubbish but every once in a while. . . Let me put it this way: no one who constantly thinks up little clever things he could/might use in a sort of stage act could possibly go on forever not thinking. Know what I mean? I try to look at life from a quite quote-unquote different perspective. I might be a bit self-unaware sometimes, a tad unversed in self-knowledge, but I'm no solipsist. I can without fear of infamy honestly say that I will listen to if not solicit the other guy's opinion—no matter how daft and outrageous and unorthodox it may be. Hahaha. (A little jest there. Touché!) Anyway, I'll put it in play form, a kind of script, you know, our fascinating-scintillating conversation, so as to amuse you. Picture us standing arms akimbo, two healthy strong fit men, sweaty, shirtless, one of them me; the other a very tall, very handsome, quite strapping, very orange-hued guy—both and all of us in fact in our diaperish underwear, the lower toga and whatnot. Manly as manly can be. You can also envision us kind of doubled over momentarily, catching our breath, bending over with our hands on our knees on account of no matter how combat-ready you are and ship-shape warriorwise, you get way winded and sore from running round using different muscles, football muscles, as it were, when you're playing football. So there were are, drinking water from a pomegranate gourd, watching our mates flash by, play out the dumb, popular game I've just told you about, our heads toggling back and forth to catch the (in)action on the field or pitch, the sharpish, excited cries of kicking and running men going round like echolalia as we (Brutus and me) converse like two noble statesmen and, eerily, seem to read each other's minds, as men at war and peasant women working weaving or threshing or washing are said to do:

ME Oh, Brutus?

BRUTUS Yes?

ME You're looking well. A bit sweaty, of course. Orangey, too.

BRUTUS Thank you, Caius. How's the old helmet? Standing you in good stead in the frays?

ME Oh, sloshing around as usual, you know. Ha! No, it's all right. I wind a cloth round my head before I put it on—like you said. You really could have given me a new one, though, and nobody'd be the worse for wear.

BRUTUS Sorry about that.

ME No worries. I say, after yesterday's bloody show, after the "sweep and clear" and all of that rot, the raping (which I don't take part in, mind) and the pillaging (which I rather *do* indulge in), I got to wondering, you know if...

BRUTUS What?

ME You ever wonder...

BRUTUS What?!

ME Never mind...

BRUTUS What? Go on, say it.

ME You won't think me possibly somewhat...seditious?

BRUTUS Not unless you say something treasonable...

ME And report me for...

BRUTUS For gods's sake, man, we're old friends! I wouldn't...

ME Okay, then. You swear?

BRUTUS Oh, for gods's sake, Caius. Out with it! Are you going to tell me that you think imperialism's major tenets and its basic ethos is or are kind of a wash or something, cruel and unnecessary; and that we should all just give up these bloody in the sense of the word "blood" campaigns and war tours and march on home to our wives and mistresses and occasional or quondam clandestine homosexual paramours? *Tush, tush*—you know what I'm saying is true! And moreover that despite the good we do for the glory of Rome you're dead sick and tired of being hacked by axes, covered with scars and sores, bedding down in swamps, intermittently malnourished, harried by foes, fleas, and fevers, dog-fatigued and nervous and anxious all the time, ready to lose it, come undone, go spare or potty, leave your last few senses, despair like mad and go howling through the camp that you can't take this anymore, that war itself is a crime, a very bad and sad thing, that humanity is horrible, and that Rome itself is a blight upon said humanity and that, ironically, despite all our propaganda, *we* are the actual barbar...

ME (shushing him a little) Keep your bleeding voice down! Okay. Right. Pretty much. I couldn't have put it more eloquently, actually. Wait...what did you say just now about...something about homosexual paramours...?

BRUTUS What? Nothing.

ME I thought you said something about homo...

BRUTUS You must have misheard me, Caius. What are you doing later tonight, by the way? Do you know where my tent, my kip, is? Come on by tonight...if you want to.

ME What?! No. No, no, no. I mean...

BRUTUS No worries. But if you should find yourself waxing insomniac...my flap is always open.

ME Your what?!

BRUTUS My tent flap. What did you think I meant?

ME Nothing. Never mind.

BRUTUS Come, come: surely you must know the talk that swirls round about these parts. About you and the Greek boy whom you let...

ME Oh my gods! That was yonks ago! I mean. Plus I was drunk. And lonely. I'm a happily married man, I am. Look here, old bean: all I wanted to talk about was some questions concerning... I mean, it *does* seem a bit arrogant to go round subduing subpar peoples who just want to get on with their filthy, vulgar, brainless, pointless, clueless, Romeless lives, doesn't it?

BRUTUS (petulantly) Whatever you say. You said it.

ME No, no, no—*you* said it.

BRUTUS Did I? I highly doubt that.

ME What?!

BRUTUS Let us say...we both did.

ME *Au contraire...*

BRUTUS (sternly) We both did.

ME Well…

BRUTUS But mostly you, come to think of it… You know I only reiterated what you exactly were thinking of telling me—in your own halting and fumbling fashion.

ME What? Get *out!* I never.

BRUTUS You know you did!

ME Get *out!* I mean…

BRUTUS (slyly) I could report you, you know…

ME You'd never!

BRUTUS (murmuring) Wouldn't I? Wouldn't I, though? See you later, maybe—Caius Aquilla?

Exit BRUTUS, walking or stalking away—not quite sure which. Ominously, a sudden rain paves the pitch. It's a real squall, a dreadful downpour. The sky crackles like a god cracking his knuckles or thumping someone on his head like a vicious and ouchy destiny. However hardy and robust, chiseled and athletic, conquering Romans do not like rain. No, no: we do not. All scramble, laughing and muddy and arm-in-arm, for the rain-sheened and dripping tents with their sopping pennants not flapping, for the warmth and comfort of their cots. All except me, for I tread dejectedly, friendless again, toward my cold and lonely bunk, with its thin pale gray blanket and full chamber pot, wondering what the Hades has just transpired so precipitately between my friend and me. I was glad of the rain, sooth to say, for I had to micturate like an *equus* used in sporting events of a racing kind, to coin a phrase. End of (sad) scenario.

P.P.S. People! I'll never understand them, Lora. What did I say to piss B off so? I wonder. *He* did all the talking, right? You read my account of our so-called conversation. I'm sort of reeling here. I really hope he's not taken serious offense or anything. After campfire tonight I tried to find him by the smithy but he was nowhere to be found. Of course I dare not look for him in his tent where he probably is. His tent like a lair of depravity. Hope you are well. Kiss the kids for me. Kiss them especially lovingly if Brutus reports me for sedition. 'Cause if he does, I'm effed completely. They crucify people for much less great offenses than that! Dear gods, let me not be crucified or even reprimanded. The worst part is that, as he (Brutus) traipsed away, I saw that Lt. Optio was standing right to our right. Brut is so big (and orange) that he was right in the line of sight, blocking anyone's view that particular way. If Optio heard wrong what was said...by me...I mean, I'm a goner: I'm in real hot water here. Oh dear, oh dear, oh dear, oh dear gods please don't let Brutus go telling anyone what we discussed.

P.P.P.S. Oh my even more serious gods, oh ye cruel, distant Olympians gazing down disinterestedly (or pointing and belly-laughing with inextinguishable laughter and mirth) on puny human lives like ours, redolent of folly and delusion, hypocrisy, duplicity, and cant! "Betrayal is the only theme!" Who said that? I did. I said that. I say it. Repeat it, too. Betrayal is the only theme! It just dawned on me that that sly, subtle, bum-banditing, nancying poofter, that faggot-fairy, flamer, and superfruity Brutus was/is threatening to blackmail me, tattle like a ten-year-old, if I don't go a-visiting him in his tent tonight. In order to let him... I can't even say it! I can't even think it! Oh woe, woe, woe, Lora. And woe again. How queer people are! What am I going to do!? Oh, Lora. I'm lost, I am. Very very effed here. I don't know what to do. What do I do, Lora? What do I do?

P.P.P.P.S. Would you be so kind, so very kind, as to, in your next (and sorry about the split infinitive), describe what a pizza tastes like? War is

Hades. It really is. I would kill—even maybe one of our own less affable fellows—for a sausage/peppers/onions/pineapple/pig with extra goat cheese plus heaps of crushed garlic and anchovies and a side of bread sticks and olive oil right now. A thin crust 'za, just a touch overcooked, with nice burnt bits, just the way I like it, as you only too well know. Yum. (*Damn* this and all wars! And my honor for a calzone or something!)

XXI APRILLUS

Dear Friend:

Hail. The special guard—two unsmiling giants I have never met, let alone seen, before—where do they get, nay, *grow* these gargantuan people, I wonder?—have just been here, to my tent, at daybreak. They didn't even knock. Well, it's not easy to knock on a tent flap, I understand, but at least they could have said, "Knock-knock" or, "Wakey-wakey!" or, "Oi, Caius Aquilla, we're come to take you to 'stand before the man' before you are shortly crucified after a swift and kangarooish court martial!" My worst fears are realized: I'm to go before the general immediately after breaking my fast. One of the giants even intimated that I would be frogmarched if I didn't come along pacifically. As if! Like I'm not going to go with them like a good soldier and warrior brave and true! Worst bit: a Roman camp breakfast's to be my final meal! Egads! What a fate! What a gyp! What a nightmare! Brutus has denounced me, surely. What else could it be? I am so screwed here. I am effed: more effed than the effed I previously thought before I was. Discombobulated, too. The general's the same one I saved from the bees or wasps! What's that mean? People's memories are so short! Has he forgotten how I lay atop him, took a stinging for him? Took several hundreds of stingings, in fact. How my poor quill quivers just the now! Lifting it, it describes nervous arabesques in the very air. It shakes and trembles like the line of craven barbarians we mowed down just the other day—a bedraggled group who were surrendering, no less. We just didn't feel like filling out the papyruswork so we just slaughtered them. Faked like we were going to let them "come over," as they say, "come in" and lay down their arms, but then we ran them through at close range. Only around thirty guys but still. Pretty dirty trick we pulled. Pretty funny, though. Could not stop laughing. Wasn't even my idea but gods a-mighty you *know* how crazy that zany Joculator gets sometimes. What a card is he! A total "idea guy," as they say. Who are "they," I always wonder? Who is this "them" people always allude to, huh? Are they a consortium of some sort, a secret society of Druids or Potentates?" Deep thoughts here. Very deep. Plus dark, disturbing, etc., which befits my current mood or mode, certes. Anyway…Lora! Gods help me—why did I ever say such compromising things before cunning-deceiving traitorous Brutus? I didn't even say them! He just read my thoughts like he was, er, reading them like a book that lay open. A book with a bookmark in it that announces "Read me!" I'm kicking myself here because why didn't I bloody go to his bloody tent last night? Maybe he just wanted a chat or summat. Maybe he just needed a friend. Yeah right: he needed a friend who'd suckle his julius or whose jules he'd suckle. I know him. I know the type. So the answer to *that* one's (why I didn't go to his tent) that there is nothing in this whole vast flat world that could ever make me be unfaithful to you, Lora, ever ever ever again—even were someone to put a freshly sharpened sword or scimitar or dagger or lance or spear or cat-o'-nine-tails to my head and fiercely-hissingly say, "Now, let this here chap suck off your julius," I would not let him. Suck me, that is. Nor I suckle him. No! I would rather die by that sword than suck or be sucked off by said imaginary guy, no matter how toothsome and irresistible.

If I have to pay for my faithfulness,

my fidelity to you,

my wife,

with my

very

life,

so be it from

Your Loving and Most Loyal (And Perhaps Quite Doomed)

Caius Aquilla

P.S. Just back from seeing the general and his frowning cronies. Braced and grimly expecting my mittimus, I marches up, I gives appropriate salute, doffs ill-fitting helmet (thanks again, Brut; thanks for nothing), in full regalia, battle gear and all the rest of it; I step in place, halt, salute again, helmet of course slipping a little on account of how sodding ill-fitting it is, and the fact that I'm nervous, sweating like a slave in the ring—and who can blame me? What I want to shout—my impulse, suppressed—is: "What the demons is this all about, General? What have I done? I've done nothing. Why am I as it were standing before the man, you being the man, the man I'm standing before, trying to suss out why I'm here, standing?" Of course I don't *say* that. But I think it so loudly that it's almost as if I have said it and a terribly guilty look traverses my visage—it must do. I must look like the fox that's been caught in the hen house with fresh yolk bearding his happy grey or red fur. Damn me. What have I done? I must have done something. Must have transgressed somehow with some transgression or other. Oh dear, oh dear, oh dear, oh dear, I'm going, thinking to myself: oh dear. Racking my brains to think what I actually did do to deserve what I anticipate to be some grotesque burlesque, me being the figure of fun. Figure of fun then tragedy, as I'm accused of high treason and sedition and disloyalty to Rome, summarily court martialed, then roundly whipped and warmly whipped, then slowly crucified in front of everyone, the lads gawking as they pass me on their way to the frays each morning, with me badly broken on the cross or wheel, sweating and drooling and bleeding, serving as a cautionary tale as my compatriots think thoughts by turns of pity, sorrow, and I-knew-this-would-happen-to-that-Caius-guy-sooner-or-later. The generals and the higher higher-ups—they don't just call you in for fun, to have a wee talk and see how you're doing, headwise; make inquiries as to how you've been holding up during the frays and if you need anything, a new sword or—hello!—helmet. Bad Brutus *has* to have ratted on me. What other explanation could there be? Ratted, yes. But about/concerning what? I never said, "We should leave these poor inferior alien personages alone and stop going about conquering them and taking their women and gold!" I never said any such thing! So, as I was telling you, I walks up. Silence at first, then a stertorous murmuring. There are four or five other high officers flanking the general, whose called Caius, as I told you. Caius Maximus, General. Who raises his hoary hand. Now it's super quiet. You could hear a goblet drop. I could use a goblet just about now. A big fat fat one that I would quaff in one go, one gulp, just *glug glug glug glug glug*—all the way down. The jingling of the horses' reigns, their mellow snorts, the wind in the pennants and the trees—these take on an eerie quality, a weird aura. The general's on a sort of a plumped-up, makeshift throne on account of he's not (as I also mentioned) tall at all. It's red and plush, the throne, with golden tassels and great candy-striped stalks of red and white. Looks really nice and comfortable. I wish I could sit in it, his chair, for just a little while. That would be grand. I've not had a good sit-down for months now. Things in the old bum dept. have not been hunky-dory ever since I was stung saving him, the ingrate! "General," says I, "you commanded me to come before you. Here I am. Here am I. As ordered." He looks down at this vast scroll he's got on his lap. He looks so bored, so over it. The bureaucracy those guys have to endure—must be tough. Not as tough as slogging through hurricanes of clayey mud to sever some Goth or Trojan's hairy head, but still. I feel for them, the officers, the generals, their staff: not an easy job, orchestrating all our maneuvers and things, deciding who gets into the thick of it, who hangs back and mops up and manifests the second wave. Lotta responsibility there. Lotta pressure. "I understand," I wanna tell him; I dream of telling him. "You don't have it easy—no matter what anyone says. None of you guys do, you who are close to the higher higher-ups. Don't let anybody tell you you have an easy, cushy job, notwithstanding the cushy cushions you've got your royal bum parked on now, mate. Honest. Even though I may have, without my knowing, done something offensive to the Legion, I can see you've taken a shine to me. A dashed shine, if I may say so. Haven't you? Well, I don't blame you. I'm quite a guy, actually. Pretty special. Extraordinary, actually. Not your usual/typical grunt. How nice if you could get to know me: I could get to know you and you could get to know me. We could have a spot of tea and a bit of a chat about things, the usual things, you know, that lowly legionaries and great, short-guy generals natter on about." "Caius Aquilla!" he intones just then, as I get to the bit, in the midst of my reveries, about the tea and chat. I give a bit of a visible start, am taken aback, as I'm a person. Startled and quite frankly gutted, I was just then, and I'm not ashamed to admit it. The mere thought of me, a distinguished legionary, here, in this predicament—the very thought of it! Insupportable. I have an unanswerable reputation, if you ask me, I do. The general's voice sounds like an oracle of oracles. Quite booming and impressive. It's a bit hard not to start and stare when a real live oracle addresses you personally, pointedly, or at least booms near you, as it did me. "Yes, sir," I says, trembling in my sandals, nearly whizzing my leather kilt. I don't mind telling you: I was intimidated. I was. Says he: "Your soldierly sojourn has been distinguished...though that is I daresay hardly the most appropriate term...by ignominy and blundering...unnecessary death and buffoonery and shame...and yet..." "Your Honor!" I says, fumbling for something to reply to this jolly sally, intending to tell him, tell him...tell him that no matter what he's heard from a certain less-than-manly party called Brutus the Orange-Colored Quartermaster I have said *nothing* treasonous, *nothing* seditious, *nothing* compromising to or of the glory of Rome, hoping to stave off whatever accusation he's going to make; assure him that whatever dread, fey Brutus told him, told on me, that is, was or is a gross distortion of...or at least just a momentary lapse of reason when...ah, I didn't know *what* I was thinking, saying... I... I... I...know I'm rather malleable sometimes and easily swayed by nefarious and attractive influences but... "Silence, blunderbuss!" the general blurted. "Where was I?" "'Shame,' Your Honor," I tells him meekly. "Right," says he and looks ferociously down at his scroll. A nice fresh small wind's making a kind of baby's plume or widow's peak of his thin blue hair. The scroll sort of lifts in the breeze and he (the general) has to sort of tamp it down so that it doesn't blow away. It looks like a papyrus swan or a pelican, one that a child might fashion after several dismal, failed attempts at it, making a bird out of paper. How I wish a great tornado or tidal wave or sudden-appearing volcano or something would come and blow us all away...spirit us away from here, wipe us out to a man (except me, of course). General Caius Maximus continues: "Shame—yes. Yet just as your career has been distinguished [again that word!], so it is now extinguished, for you are granted, it says here, three months leave." "What?!" I say. "Just what I said," the general announces and calls me over with a little clap-cupping of the fingers of his free hand. "See here—'**Caius Aquila: leave granted for three months.**' Go on, man. There's a viaticum and a wagon waiting for you to take you to the city of Nice, from whence you will embark on an expensive delicate ship, sojourn upon the seas, then dock in Ostia and be home in glorious Rome in no time. This *is* you, isn't it?" The general bids me crane and look. There it is:

'Caius Aquila.' One "l," not two. Must be some other bloke. Someone who is not I. How can that be? The Roman Imperial never makes mistakes like this! Not in a million thousand moons! What a terrific serendipity! What an hoot. He (the general) points with his shaking (has he been at the palm wine already this fair morning?), authoritative finger to the column on the left of the scroll. On the right hand side, glancing, I see something quite shocking: "Caius Aquilla" is the name that's calligraphied there. It's a list of casualties. Fatalities, no less. *I'm dead!* Well at least the list says so. Where did they get *that* idea from? Wait! Joc, maybe?! It'd be just like him, for a larf, to report me as dead, a fatality! I thought I *was* going to die, be court martialed and crucified, and it turns out there's something better for me: I'm dead! They think I died in combat! More fools them! I mean, the last few frays have been inordinately tough, but nothing out of the ordinary for a noble Roman such as Yours Truly, Your Caius. I am dead! I *am* dead! If that makes sense. (It doesn't.) No more does this recent and utterly unexpected development. Goes to show you: you never know. How odd life is. I've hardly had a scratch for weeks! It must've been the other Caius A. who's gone and croaked it, and just on the eve of his leave, too, and some orderly misspelled his name! Dear gods, *I'm going home, Lora! I'm coming home to you.* They've made a grave (pun!) mistake. I'm outta here! I may never have to come back! Huzzah, hurrah for me! I go from quaking with fear to jumping for joy. I try to conceal my peeing-in-my-kit/kilt excitement and sort of nobly nod when the general asks me if that's me. Ha! I never said it was; just the nod was enough. I could have been about to sneeze or something. My honor, my integrity—*I* think—is intact. And besides, they'll never figure their error, military bureaucracy being what it foully is this days, FUBAR and all of that, don't you know. Well, well, well. Gotta pack my kit up ASAP before they find it's a clerical and orthological error! Which they never will! Better stop writing now and get on that bus! Well, not a bus but you know what I mean! Mwah and see you soon from

Your Caius "Aquila"!

P.S. Hahaha. Wonderful!!!!

XXI MAIUS

Dear Friend:

We've had a quite quiet time here. Have not heard from you for over a month now. I do hope you're "alright" as they're spelling it these dark orthological days when just about anything goes, orthologically. Preposterous. Let's see. What's new with us? Julia's lost another tooth. She does jar her mouth so the way she jumps up & down monomaniacally-neurotically. Wonder what is up with that? Furthermore, she often puts (or tries to, anyway) her entire fist in her mouth. I wonder if she'll be an artist or something. I have heard oracles & soothsayers say that that's the sort of strange behavior great sculptors & painters exhibit when young. When old, as well, but no matter. An oral fixation, they called it—sure to result in eventual genius. I'm sure she's fine, Julia. Aurelian, contrapuntally, makes great progress in his studies & sword fighting lessons. Your five sisters were here for high tea the other day, as was Drusilla & her dullard children—for a playdate that went entirely wrong as Julia & Aurelian retreated to their chambers at the very thought of Dru's kids. Such snobs, bless their exclusive little hearts. Most chuffed to see them do that. Me smiling & bursting with pride to know we've raised them well, instilled in them the proper virtues of eschewing "Not Our Kind, Dear" types & playfellows who are—let's be honest—beneath them. I invited Dru & brood on account of even though I've known them for forever, that quintet of strumpets who are related to you, I just can't relate to them, find myself clamming up whenever they turn up. Nothing, absolutely nothing, in common save you, Caius Aquilla. Hence no conversation to speak of. I thought I'd invite Drusilla & a few of her friends & make it a real live old fashioned hen house for an afternoon. A ladies only free-for-all. It was quite the success, I daresay. Everybody laughed & gossiped like mad & talked their silly heads off & gobbled enormous amounts of cake & pig & candied cow & sugar cane & glugged many-a-hogshead of our best vintages—I think I can safely say we've been eaten out of house & home. How marvelous. Terrific party. Just the thing. I adored it—for a little while, that is. It was easy enough for me, after an hour or so, to slip away & get some writing down, done. My little novel writing exercise (I think you'd call it) is coming along amazingly, I think. Swimmingly. If I do say so myself. & I do. I do. The hard parts, I suppose, are your letters—me pretending to be you & all. I have no very difficult time pretending to be *me*, but you—that's another story, as they say. It's been quite an adventure, imagining your camp life & the unparalleled comraderie & the frays & politics & alliances & homosexual overtones of the Royal Imperial Roman Army & things. All that subtext & so forth. Male bonding qua repressed faggotry. Simply gripping, though—that's certain. Dreaming it up as we artist-scribblers do. Otherwise, as for life at home, it goes as may be expected, it goes on apace, the quotidian routine, the daily grind & all of that: I read, write, eat, & drink, eat, drink unapologetically & to excess, as you might expect. The lyre (harp) master's just been here & given me my weekly lesson. Such a nice chap. Well, as he's blind as a bat I reckon he has to be. Can't imagine an imperious & hectoring sightless fellow! Absurd! What sort of hissy fit could he throw?! Gets all huffy and dictatorial (as most music masters do) & everybody just leaves the room, snickering & pointing at his blind ass. Or they pin a note on his back, unbeknownst to him, that says, "Fool!" or, "Blind Bloody Fool!" or, "Look out, angry blind harping guy here—he'll start yelling at you if you don't watch yourself!" Hahaha. I've made some progress, harpwise. Right best pleased about it, too. I can't say I'm a virtuoso or anything & ready to try for The Senate Orchestra, but I am pretty good now, quite the accomplished accompanist! Can't wait to play you some new songs plus a few new things with you when you return, dear friend. I do miss playing music with you, husband. Among other things, *playwise*, if you know what I mean! *Assplay*, is what I mean, Caius—pure & simple. Or not so pure & not so simple. I feel I must spell it out for you. I need to be made love to so badly, Caius. I need carnal relations & no mistake. Gone down on, ravished, thrown up against a plinth or wall, the full nine. It's been so so so long. I'm feeling so so so frisky right now. I'm going to stop here, fetch my leathern stick &, well, you know...plunge it into me & think of you having me from behind. Wait! What's that? What did I just hear? Did I just hear the servants announce, "The Master!" "The Master's here! The Master's home!" did they just say? Did I hear that a-right? I can't believe my ears. & hope not to believe my very eyes in a sec here! My word, my gods, Caius! Is that really you standing there in our courtyard with giant grin on your sweet face & a huge bouquet of gold and purple flowers in one beautifully scarred & war-roughened hand & your trusty lute in the other?! Is that a purple trunkful of spoils, of glory & plunder, at your triumphant feet? Are you really come back without a monkey or an orangutan this time? How extraordinary! Blessed be the gods, thrice blessed our house! Are darling Aurelian & little Julia really & truly shrieking like mad banshees & running toward you just the now, throwing themselves into your ever so strong & homecoming arms? Caius! Are you really home? Or am I dreaming?! My Caius Aquilla, husband, dear friend, old chap, old top...can that really be you?!

Two days later, in full ceremonial regalia, a superannuated messenger from the Imperial Roman Army (quite stout, most begrizzled, to all appearances someone who seemed as though he suffered from severe lower back pain) arrived at the enormous wooden-of-course gates of the Aquilla homestead courtyard. Aurelian—who was shooting little colored pebbles at some of the bigger domestic courtyard animals, chasing them round and round, having at them with a little purple catapult—shoved aside the doddering porter and answered the man's ominous knock; then signed for the red wax-sealed and signet-stamped scroll the legionary emissary handed him. It was addressed to The Honorable Mrs. Dame Caius Aquilla, Widow. Dropping his wee weapon, running holding the communication like an anchorman in a relay race, Aurelian darted into the cool central family room, skidded kiddily past the servants punkahwallahing there with sizeable palm fronds, kiddily and ostentatiously—plus ululating like a barbarian, and handed his mummy the crackling papyrus. "Aurelian, whatever are you raving about?" Lora Cecilia said. "Mummy! Mummy!" Aurelian hollered. "Look what's come for you!" Lora gazed up at him, her brilliant-shining perfect son, then unceremoniously hove or heaved little Julia off her lap. They'd been sitting on the plush red couch, thumbing and nodding through a charming oversize baby blue picture book of dangerous and venomous animals and fascinating poisonous plants. As Caius, sensing momentous events or messages afoot, padded in to said room (toweling off from having soaked himself in one of the baths for nigh-on two hours, as good Romans, in hail-the-conquering-hero mode will do), Lora smiled widely and said: "Oh look, husband-dear! News of your untimely, valiant, and heroic death has just arrived!" "Huzzah!" Caius cried. "Hurrah!" Caius cried. "Hooray, hooray!" Aurelian shouted and picked up from where it was lying on a zebra rug his gold and silver wooden sword and held it up in tribute. "He's dwead, he's dwead, he's dwead!" little Julia ejaculated, and jumped her lunatic jump, up and down and up and down and up and down and up and down.

THE END